FALLING SNOW ON SNOW

Falling Snow on Snow © 2016 by Lou Sylvre.
Cover Art © 2019 by Loretta Sylvestre

Published 2020 by Rainbow-Gate Romance

(First Edition: Dreamspinner Press, Tallahassee, FL 2016)

# Falling Snow on Snow

## Seattle, Music, Snow, Love

LOU SYLVRE

Rainbow Gate Romance

*To musicians, to veterans, and to those who*
*light candles on December nights*

# CONTENTS

*"Of course the music is a great difficulty. You see, if one plays good music, people don't listen, and if one plays bad music people don't talk."*
—Oscar Wilde

*"Laughter is the sun that drives winter from the human face."*
—Victor Hugo

~ 1 ~

CHAPTER ONE

Beck's gray blankets were vintage Army surplus wool, and if he thought about it, they itched. But they kept him warm, and that was still a miracle for him, so he slept well under them, and even when he did notice the itch, he didn't grouse about it. It hadn't been so very long since those two blankets were *all* that lay between him and winter's killing cold.

Now the old clock he'd bought at Goodwill squealed its alarm, and Beck rolled out from under the covers and off the Murphy bed that constituted the epitome of luxury in his mind. As he did every morning, he padded on stockinged feet into the kitchen, plucked a bowl of yesterday's nonreusable leftovers from the fridge, and took it up to a hidden corner on the roof. King Coal, the one-footed crow he'd befriended, would dine on it at leisure. Beck wasn't sure how, but the old black bird kept all the competition at bay, claiming Beck's daily offering for himself as if it was some sort of tribute. It made Beck smile, though, to see the down-and-out bird prosper.

At 5:45 a.m., the winter morning remained every bit

as dark as night. Despite the frigid air, Beck stayed on the roof for a few minutes to take in the view. He could see to the high-rises across Lake Union from his vantage, but what he paid attention to were the nearby back-yards—each one seeming shabbier than the next—and the myriad windows in the four- and five-story apartment buildings that dotted the neighborhood.

Holiday lights burned in many of those windows, mostly left on all night. If he'd been a violent sort, he would have wanted to throw things, shatter the windows in an effort to cut the cords that kept them lit.

*Beck*, he told himself, *you would think they were pretty if they weren't about the holidays.*

*I fucking hate Christmas. I fucking hate December. Ergo I hate the fucking lights.*

Pretty sure it would be bad karma to start the day on such a negative note, he reminded himself out loud, "But you know what? I have an apartment!" In fact, he had two hundred square feet of studio apartment living space, with a microwave, a fridge, a bed, a shower. And—more importantly—a roof between him and Seattle's cold rain.

Back inside, he pulled the window shades to shut out the chill, the dark, and the deceptively pretty holiday lights, and then switched on the wall heater, savoring the instantaneous desert wind hitting his ankles and knees.

"Parcheesi!" he called softly a few minutes later. "Come get breakfast, cat!"

He filled her kibble, gave her clean water, and dutifully scratched her fur, the color of which reminded him he actually had a small jar of marmalade in the fridge.

Breakfast, then. Instant coffee and noninstant oatmeal with canned milk, a few raisins, and a pat of butter—all of which came to him compliments of the King County food bank—and a teaspoonful of the marmalade, which he'd splurged for after he'd scored his permit to perform inside Pike Place Market. While he sat near the heater and ate, he studied the marbled oranges and yellows of the preserve. *Summer in a jar*, he thought, which warmed him, made him smile, and let him forget the season and all its phony glitz for just a few seconds.

He was glad he'd bought the marmalade, which had been a "today only" special at the Hilltop Safeway. Usually, he saved his limited food cash for lunches, which he'd eat during a break from the long days he worked playing his guitar for donations at Pike Place Market.

He loved playing music—it kept him alive. And he loved not having to cower under a sidewalk awning outside in the cold to play it. He loved that the people passing by in the market were a bit more likely to toss him some coin than the ones on the street—especially the tourists. Lots of tourists in the market.

But he didn't love the job. Not right now.

*December.*

*Figgie pudding, red-nosed reindeer, kings of orient, barumpa bum bum, on the fucking housetop.*

He played the season's music, the songs full of family and false cheer, because that's what the shoppers wanted. It was what people would pay for this time of year, but every "Jingle Bells" and "Joy to the World" grated on him. There was nothing all that joyful about Christmas, and probably not Hanukkah or Kwanzaa or Ramadan and Eid—though he knew less about how people celebrated those. Being honest with himself, Beck admitted the existence of quite a lot of "holy day" music he loved even though he professed no religion. Old chant, liturgical hymns. Those held a kind of peace, or sometimes poignant longing that reached his heart. But if he played those, he wouldn't be able to pay the rent. Occasionally he got a request for "The Dreidel Song" or "Oh Kwanzaa," which was a change of pace, at least, but people didn't want to shop to the tune of "Maoz Tzur" or "As I Lay on Yoolis Night," beautiful though they were.

Regardless of which holiday was front and center, Beck knew December had the blackest heart of any month. The days came cold and dreary more often than not, and shopping bags might be full of pretty things, but he felt sure they were empty of anything resembling humanity and compassion. He happened to know those smiling, gift-laden daddies and grandmothers easily passed right by broken children on the street without a second glance.

*Beck Justice! You're being negative again. Stop. You have a lot less to bitch about than you did last year, you know.*

"Yes," he agreed with himself, and told the supremely disinterested Parcheesi, "We have an apartment. Lucky, right?"

She mewed, and he took that as assent. After all, Parcheesi had been homeless too.

As he luxuriated in the rich extravagance commonly called a hot shower, he let his mind wander to thoughts of the gnarly, tightfisted old man whose improbable kindness led to Beck acquiring this apartment near Twenty-Third and Denny Way, his very own tiny urban paradise.

Tracing good fortune back to its source, Beck owed his shelter, his full stomach, his warm clothes, and his ability to pay for these things to the secret kindness of one unlikely individual, Dooley, of Dooley's Pawn and Loan. Dooley's shop fronted Sixteenth Avenue in White Center, one of the economic low points in the greater Seattle area. Along with the other shops in the block, its brick façade had seen brighter days, and the display windows were crammed with a variety of obsolete electronics, beer steins and bric-a-brac, musical instruments, and power tools. Of course, Dooley's real money came from the business he did in guns, and he had a decided knack for knowing when to lose the paperwork on those. His tendency to be tightfisted with a loan didn't hurt his bottom line either, nor did his policy of never holding something a single day longer as collateral than he had to. If you were late to pick up your pawn, you paid the selling price—no second chances.

A lot of people Beck met on the street didn't like Dooley one bit, and that seemed perfectly understandable. Yet when the crusty older man found Beck shivering through a frigid predawn February morning under some cardboard in the gravel behind his shop, he'd taken him inside and given him coffee. And gloves. And a pack of saltines with a tin of sardines.

"Come back tonight. Half past five. Clean the place up. Sleep in the storeroom."

Instead of saying thanks, Beck asked, "You trust me?"

"No trustin' about it. You gonna be locked in. Cain't get out lest you set off the alarm. Ain't gettin' away with a damn thing."

Beck never had to sleep outside again. Soon he was working for Dooley almost full-time, and Dooley paid him cash money. With an address, he was able to get medical benefits and food, and every day he got stronger. When Dooley said, "Time for you to move on, boy. You been gettin' 'spensive," Beck had nothing but gratitude for what the gnarly old man had given him, and at that point, he was ready for a change. He bought a banged-up but beautiful Seagull Coastline folk guitar from Dooley at about half what someone else would pay, and spent the rest of his hoarded cash on the deposit and two months' rent for his tiny but perfect apartment.

Then he started peddling his music on the streets.

That had been right at summer's end, a fair-weather time of year in the Puget Sound region, and Seattle was both generous and an outdoors kind of town. Beck sought out lucrative spots day by day, parking himself just outside a festival one day, on a busy street corner the next. A few times, a tavern owner called him inside to play for the weeknight patrons, payment coming in the form of a meal and tips. He would play mostly blues then, wringing truth from his beat-up acoustic with things like "Black Mountain Rag," changing it up with Clapton's "Tears in Heaven" or Neil Young's beautifully sad "Birds." The weather held right through October, and the world had generally treated Beck well. And in November, after he got the chance to start playing in the Market, he woke one Thursday morning to find his zest for life had returned.

Too bad December came snapping at November's heels.

Just as Beck was mentally shoring up his resolve with a pledge to outlast the hated holiday month, the shower went suddenly cold, and Beck cursed his carelessness. He knew the hot water would spend itself in about four minutes now that a hard frost happened more nights than not. If he didn't want to be shocked out of his reverie with a cold blast, he couldn't afford a retreat to memories while showering.

*At least they were the better memories this time, not the bitter ones.*

Following close on that thought, some of those unsavory recollections threatened to play themselves out in his mind, but he shut them down, pushed them back. Thoughts of his parents, of being young and on the streets, thoughts of a beautiful, treacherous lover named George—they'd all have to wait. He'd never survive through the month of merriment if he let himself tumble down into the dark places.

He stepped out of the shower, stood in front of the heater to quickly dry and dress, and sat on the bed with his guitar.

Gently strumming through a few undeliberate chords, he gazed out the tall window and drank in the muted sunrise. Heavy gray clouds banked over the city as usual, but a haze of golden sunshine snuck beneath them. *No matter the season*, it seemed to say, *summer is always coming.*

Beck laughed aloud and, after calming the startled

Parcheesi with a few chin scratches, began to play. Inspired by the thought of summer, he wove melody over a base line, rendering "Sumer is a Cumin In," which most people who'd ever heard of it at all thought of as "The Cuckoo Song." The title wasn't misspelled; it was old. Thirteenth century old.

When it came to music, Beck had lots of favorites—blues, slack key, classical, acoustic rock. Whatever seemed like the right thing to play took the role of favorite for the moment, and this morning, it was the hollow harmonies and complicated, wavering and jumping melodies of the Middle Ages. As strange as it seemed, this music had been a gift of his years on the streets.

He'd been sixteen when he first heard it, on a night when he'd snuggled into the blankets he'd laid out in the shrubs behind Trinity Episcopal. Earlier he'd picked up a recent copy of *The Stranger* and was leafing through it in the last light of the late September day when he heard singing. Not just any singing. Voices like something from another world. It was only a group of local women—the Medieval Women's choir—but he didn't know that then, and the sound came to him so pure that tears came to his eyes. He'd started loving early music that day, and every chance he got after that, he played it—by ear at first, and then he started spending his coins on yellowed, cracking sheet music from thrift stores and secondhand bookshops.

Beck couldn't sing—carrying a tune was all well and good, but his voice had been ruined by a near fatal bout of pneumonia during his second winter on the streets. His guitar *could* sing, though, and it rendered those ancient melodies in graceful, shining lines of silver and gold whenever Beck's fingers asked it. This morning he started slowly, remembering as he often did that someone—he could never find out who—had famously said "Make love to every note." It seemed apt, though it reminded him annoyingly that playing notes on his guitar was the only lovemaking he was likely to do these days. He played through "Danger Me Hath, Unskylfuly" and "Blow, North-erne Wynd" before thoughts of Christmas flash-and-bang sent him back to the blues, and they carried him through until it was time to pack up his guitar and go.

After the cold and damp of the fifteen-minute walk to Pike Street, he splurged on hot coffee and walked around the market window-shopping, greeting the few fellow performers who were there at the early hour, and warm-ing up his muscles before he found his first spot for the day and set up.

# ~ 2 ~

## CHAPTER TWO

That day and each day that week, Beck slogged to the market through the rain, warmed up his hands, and quenched his resentments for ten hours, eight or so of which he played Christmas carols, smiled at tippers, joked with overburdened shoppers, and encouraged little children to sing along with "Rudolph the Red-Nosed Reindeer." Etcetera. After an hour in one spot, he and every performer was required to move on and let the next busker in line take the spot. Sometimes he could move right to another location, but sometimes that meant he had to be in the queue for an hour before he could settle in to play again. Occasionally he'd spend the hour window-shopping or people watching, but neither activity was good for his mood, so he always brought a book.

When George had left him for greener pastures—green as in money—he'd left behind a few things. Not much, because while they'd been together, they'd mostly lived—like many of the homeless—in one or another of the tent cities in Seattle, and it was hard to accumulate much in the way of belongings while living that kind of life. The villages of tents weren't permanent, and when the lease was up, so to speak, a person had to be ready to move on. But George had liked to read when he wasn't panhandling, and he'd amassed a paperback fortune consisting of *Lord of the Rings*, three of Jane Austen's novels, and eleven gay romances.

Beck hadn't read any of them while George was still around. Still, for inexplicable reasons, he'd schlepped them around with him during the months between George's desertion and Dooley's rescue, and when he got his apartment, he'd made a shelf for them next to his bed out of a plastic crate he'd found at Value Village, and then he'd finally started reading them. Having individual love-hate relationships with each of the books, he was currently working his way through them for the third time.

He liked the way he fell in love with the characters every time. He dreaded the way he felt so much more alone when he reached the end.

On a break during Thursday that week, he finished one, and consequently he felt irritable, unsettled, and basically shitty. Then he started to play, and if it wasn't bad enough he had to play trite Christmas songs, some smartass designer-shoe-wearing teenager had started hollering lyrics at the top of his unpleasant voice, driving away anybody who might have been tempted to toss a few bills into his guitar case. So when at that moment George came strolling by on the arm of some uptown old man and, without even a nod Beck's way, tossed a bill into his case, Beck's mood turned black as coal dust. He wanted to shout at George to keep his damn money. He wanted to grab the bill and catch up with George and rip it up in his face.

If it had been a dollar bill, or maybe even a five, a ten, he would have done it. But it was a damn fifty-dollar bill, and Beck could not afford to feed his pride at the expense of his belly. He plucked the bill from the hoard and stuck it in his sock—*like the music whore I am.*

That night it snowed, big flakes falling all around Beck as he made the trek back to his tiny, warm home, white silence tamping his bright ire into sullen pain. Wool blankets pulled over his head like a cowl and wrapped like a shroud, he stood on the roof watching the frantic march of the holiday city slow to an obliging crawl, the people bowing in their unprepared surprise to the weather's superior forces. Back inside, he left the lamps off and sat on his bed cross-legged—Parcheesi taking advantage of his lap—and stared out through the window, wondering what he thought he might see.

Snow in Seattle is often an ephemeral thing, covering the city by night, gone by day. But this time, contrary to predictions, it not only remained but kept falling, creating sledding hills out of residential streets and blocking doorways with drifts. On Friday, the shoppers still came to the Market, and Christmas music proceeded to echo through the halls, including that produced by Beck's guitar. If anything, the people were a little less hurried, maybe their smiles a bit more genuine, but they still wanted "White Christmas" and "Jingle Bells," and Beck didn't think any real goodness resided at the heart of the holiday season, whether white or blue or even rainbow.

The snow stopped Friday afternoon, but started again in the silver dawn Saturday morning, and that day the Market seemed as whisper quiet as the rest of the city. Around four in the afternoon, Beck was performing in one of the Market's coldest and generally least bustling corners. Of the few people passing by, not one stopped to listen, and Beck's fingers responded of their own accord by simply stopping. He sat down in the corner, his back against the wall, and looked out a long window opposite. The sun shone momentarily, its isolated orange rays slanting through the falling flakes as if giving a wave to remind the city it still burned. The sight was mesmerizing, and Beck didn't think at all before he started to play a song he loved—a song of a Christmas day grim and harsh, one which, unlike storefronts and Santa photos, might harbor true compassion.

Beck's fingers coaxed a dark, cold wind from the strings, and he felt the words of the hymn he played rise in his throat and form on his tongue. He let them loose, speaking them like a poem of loneliness, and left them hanging in the air on frozen breath.

"In the bleak midwinter frosty winds made moan.

Earth was hard as iron, water like a stone."

He wanted to stop the words. They made the music more beautiful, more true than ever, and he wanted to listen to it, to hear what his hands were telling him. This wasn't the kind of music to play to a Christmas-shopping crowd at Pike Place Market—he knew that. Yet where moments before no one had even looked at his happy caroling guitar as they passed—even if they tossed money into his open case—now he saw through the screen of his eyelashes that people gathered. They waited for something, a small crowd still as a deep winter night.

Despite his reluctance, his words continued to steal out into the world as if they had every right to his voice, but then he heard something else. At first he thought it an echo—the market was full of them—but it gained in strength and beauty, and he understood. Someone had begun to sing. Clear, brave, flawless as Beneventan chant.

Like an angel in a cathedral.

His own words became a whisper, his fingers grew more sincere as they traveled the strings in pursuit of a beauty that would match the singer's voice. He lifted his gaze to search the small crowd that had gathered, but not one among the men, women, or children moved their lips or seemed to do anything but listen, perhaps as enchanted as he was by the sounds. It seemed a moment touched by something beyond the mundane, and he thought of his grandmother's rosary hanging as always around his neck, though it meant nothing religious to him at all.

Beck wasn't, in fact, a man of religion. And though he admitted the possibility that something more existed than what could be seen, the closest he knew to spirit lived right there, in the music. In the tones born in the body of a fine guitar, the passage of breath through the vein of a flute. In the flight of sound on the wings of a perfect voice. Like this one.

"Snow was falling, snow on snow." The singer wove the words over and under the harmonies Beck offered up with fingers and strings, turned them into something different, something *more*.

The song ended, as all songs do. But this time, when the words stopped and the echoes died away, Beck felt a thrill of panic, for he still hadn't located the person who'd been singing. What if he never found the singer, never again heard that soaring voice, never looked into the eyes of the man who sang. *Yes*, he thought, *a man*. He hadn't been sure at first, as the alto voice had reached notes high for the range. *But it's a man*, he thought again, and he knew it because of the way the voice had touched him.

He stood and again scanned the crowd. He asked an older couple standing near, "Did you see who was singing?"

They shook their heads, but the woman smiled gently, as if the soul-deep need he felt could be seen on his face, heard in the phrasing of his question. He tried to smile back.

As quickly as he could, he gently laid his guitar in its case and ran. He rounded the corner of the shop and looked up the long, dimly lit hall that sloped up to the next level of the market. A slender man in jeans, with long, curling hair and a loose flannel shirt trailing behind him like a cape, strode quickly away. *It's him!*

"Wait!" Beck called, and the man half turned as if to obey, but instead spun back around and kept moving. Away from Beck. He turned a corner at the top and was lost to sight. Beck warred with himself—he wanted to follow and find him, needed to. But he also needed to eat and pay rent. If he followed his heart, the money people had tossed in his guitar case wouldn't be there when he came back. Nor would his instrument, his livelihood, his only means of staving off damp cold and gnawing hunger. So he turned back, picked up his Seagull, and began a catchy rhythm for "Up on the Housetop."

He didn't care about "Up on the Housetop," and though people were smiling and tossing money in the case, he had never been more certain that Christmas was nothing more than hype and a good sales strategy. "Bah," he muttered into his instrument. "Humbug."

Except. Somewhere out there was a man with an angel's voice.

*Gone. Like everyone else. I'll never see him again.*

All thought of going upstairs for coffee fled Oleg's mind, though that had been the whole reason he'd come through the Market this morning on his way home. He wrapped his smelly shirt close around him and started to run. He felt completely stupid doing it, but he didn't stop until he was sure he'd lost his pursuer.

*What am I running from?*

Oleg had no sensible answer. The man with the guitar was just that, a man, and the devil could testify Oleg didn't usually run from an interested man—especially not one who looked like the guitarist. All long legs and strong hands and s-e-x from head to toe.

Which is what Oleg thought he himself probably smelled like—sex. He'd "gone out" the previous night. "Out" was where he told his family he was going when he went prowling bars for someone who'd hold him tight, who'd touch him, need him, *want* him. Someone who'd fuck his brain quiet and satiate the longing he was never free of for long.

The first man he'd picked up last night had only wanted to fuck in the car. The sex was hot and quick, as sex in semipublic places tended to be, but the encounter didn't even rattle the empty spaces. The second of the night had gone a little better. The man—who said his name was Jim—took him home to a spacious apartment near Broadway and fucked him good for an hour, then fell into a coma-like sleep. Oleg had stayed, though he hadn't slept much, fantasizing instead that this encounter wasn't more of the usual, that the man who slept beside him hadn't simply *forgotten* to kick him out the door before he fell asleep. But in the morning, Oleg realized—even before Jim showed him the door—that he didn't even like the guy, with all his cold, sharp-edged décor and heavy gold jewelry.

That, in fact, was the problem with the overnight kind of hookup. If he let them—and he always did—they could *seem* to sate more than sex drive. In truth the encounter with Jim was no different than the car-fuck, except he had farther to fall back down when it was over. True to form, by the time Seattle's rare December snow cooled the sex memory off him, Oleg was lonely again.

*Lonely.*

Most of the time, he didn't like to think that's what he was. He was a lucky guy; he knew that. He had a big, loving, accepting family, and all of them had more to be thankful for than many. They'd come from cold, hungry Russia in the 1990s, and unlike most refugees they had what were called by the welfare people they'd had to depend on when they first arrived, "marketable skills."

What the family had was music, and it had opened so many doors for them. Now they had made their name in early music circles, had regular bookings for concerts and special appearances as a group and individually, and they had a home. Warm, large but not so much so that it ever felt *too* spacious. Never empty. Air rich with the smells of stroganoff, borscht, shashlik, or honeycake. Ready laughter, flash-in-the-pan tempers, small favors asked or done. And behind it all, in the Abramov home, always the music: scales ad infinitum, students repeating sixteen measures over and over slow to fast and finally tumbling into the following passage. Sometimes, too, whole beautifully sculpted pieces, perilous to the listening—or performing—heart.

Home, for Oleg Andreyevich Abramov was a luck-laden word indeed, for in Russia, beloved though the country might be in some ways, the family had endured cold and hunger and hate—the former because of political and economic collapse, the latter mostly because Andrei, Oleg's father, was Jewish. Oleg, youngest by nine years, had only faint memories of the old country. A grandmother sang "Dreidel, Dreidel, Dreidel." A tiny room held only a bed, where a faded and frayed diamond quilt of velvet, silk, and wool warded Oleg and his brothers against winter. Snowdrifts loomed taller than a little boy. His mother's hands gamboled over the keys of a scratched piano. His uncle spun him in circles, smelling of bow rosin and lavender.

But distant and dim as those memories might be, they

remained very much a part of Oleg, because the Abramovs had brought the old country with them to Seattle. The mild climate had done nothing to dispel the sense that a family huddled tight together would weather any storm.

One might have expected such a family to resent a child—the youngest and all but a straggler—who was *different*. But when Oleg had told his mother he was gay, she'd accepted it.

"Yes, I believe I already knew," she said, her gently accented speech conveying as always a love of life's surprises. "Or at least I should have." She laughed and hugged him and set the tone of acceptance for the family. It persisted even now, after her death. He remained their *Olejka*, a precious member of the family.

Yes, his life was full of *home*—meaning love and warmth and acceptance.

But that didn't eliminate the longing. Maybe, it changed the shape of the emptiness, made it even harder to fill. Because Oleg wanted more of what he already had. He wanted a man who loved him, who would take him wholesale into his life and also be willing and able to weave himself seamlessly into Oleg's family.

"You look in the wrong places!" That had been part of his mother's last words to him.

He'd entered her room where she lay propped on a mound of stark white pillows. She had chosen to fight the pain of her tumors and remain conscious for a last private talk with each of her loved ones.

"Mom," he'd said, the most American of her offspring, and sat on the edge of her bed, carefully taking her small, bone-thin hand in his. He'd wanted her to embrace him, but knew she didn't have the strength. He kissed her forehead, and she smiled. As he straightened, she fixed her dark brown, remotely Asian eyes on him and spoke, her voice low, her accent spread thicker than ever over the English words.

"Son, I know what you do, the nights you leave us. I can smell the liquor on you, and yes, the men."

Alarm shot through him. He'd thought he was circumspect, careful, never coming home drunk or with his clothing too much in disarray. "Mom, I'm sorry—"

She cut him off, momentarily stern. "No need, no time. Listen. What you are finding is not what you are looking for, in your heart. What you are looking for is not easy to find, but also not impossible. But Oleg, you are looking in the wrong places!"

Oleg had wanted to redeem himself in her eyes. "Mom, some really great people hang out at bars, clubs. Nice men. People you'd like."

"Of course, Olejka," she said, seeming energized by fond frustration. "But I know you do not go to find friends and conversation. And don't look so shocked. I am *praktichnaya jenchina*! Practical woman, yes? Good eyes, smart brain, and I've... how do you say it? Been around the corner?"

Oleg had to smile, but in the face of losing his mother, the affection in that expression gave way to grief, and by the time he spoke, he had to push the words through tears. "The block, Mom," he managed. "You've been around the block."

She stopped speaking then, panting and breaking out in sweat from what must have been a sudden flare of the ever-present pain. After a moment, the spasm seemed to pass, and she fixed her failing gaze on Oleg once more. "You do not go for the friends, my son. It is not easy for you, the talking, the *obshcheniye*... friendly drink. You go alone. You come home, you are loneliest. Always."

She closed her eyes. Oleg squeezed her hand gently, sorry for exhausting her. She found the strength to squeeze back but kept her eyes closed as she spoke. "The places are fine, Oleg. But for your looking? They are not... useful."

Quiet fell between them, lasting exactly eleven of his mother's breaths—Oleg counted them. When she spoke again, it was only to tell him that he, her youngest, her surprise child, remained always precious to her, and her love would remain with him despite death's separation.

And then the audience was over. "Send in your sister Lara now, Olejka."

He thought about her insight now, more than a year since, as he fled down the back stairs of the market and stepped out into the chill weather on traffic-snarled Western Avenue. He wrapped his flannel shirt tight around him and bent his head against the wind as he walked around to Third and Virginia to catch the bus, which would take him home to the Greenwood neighborhood, a place that bore no resemblance to the bars on Broadway at all. He'd be safe there, almost smothered with love, and he wouldn't have to think about why he was running away from the man with the guitar.

Oleg had enough insight into his own mind and heart to know what his mother had said was true—had known it even before hearing it from her mouth. But the facts remained. He saw the people that went to the bars for simple camaraderie—often couples, sometimes just friends. He didn't know how to become that, and it wasn't why he went there. And always—after a few drinks—the hookups, the sloppy kisses and minimalist sex, the indulgent and dangerous self-deceptions all became easy. Today, letting his voice float through the market suspended in the lovely chorded tones of the beautiful man's guitar had been easy too, natural.

But talking to a man like the guitarist was not.

Now, stinking of last night's booze and sex times two, wearing the crumpled, sweaty clothes he'd worn through dancing, drinking, and car sex and finally picked up off a stranger's floor, such a thing as turning around to meet the guitarist wasn't even possible.

Poorly clad for the weather, he dashed through the snow and met the bus just as it arrived. After flashing his metro pass, he made his way toward the back. Glad to see for once there was a seat available, he swung into it and sat down more heavily than he'd intended.

*I'll probably never see him again.*

He closed his eyes on the discouraged, empty way that thought made him feel and let himself drift into a light doze filled with the faint imagined sound of snowfall, and of arpeggios becoming fingers playing lightly through his hair.

He jerked awake just in time for his stop, sure as if he'd

set an alarm. Back out in the cold, walking the one-block distance to his house, he wondered if the snow would stay for Christmas.

As soon as he got inside his over-the-garage room at the family home, he pulled the blinds, stripped his smelly clothes, and stepped into a long, hot shower. The difference in the way he felt before and after amazed him, even though he'd been through precisely this transformation dozens of times before. Shaved and combed, dressed now in clothes that were much the same as what he'd worn before but clean and soft and not at all grungy, he smiled forgiveness at himself in the mirror.

He stepped out into the weather once more for the twenty steps it took to get to the back door of the house, then slipped inside to the homey warmth of the kitchen, where Lara was heating water for tea. When she turned to greet him, he saw inconvenient knowledge in her eyes, accompanied by fathomless compassion. She set down the worn dish towel she'd been drying her hands with and drew him into a hug. Suddenly Oleg's heart felt heavy as stone. He clung to her, this older sister who always understood him, not letting go until he'd quashed the lump in his throat and the burn in his eyes.

"You should stop, Oleg. This thing you do brings you nothing good." As always when she mothered him, her accent thickened until she sounded more like their mother than herself.

He nodded, saying nothing, and accepted the offered tea glass. She put a plate of pirozhki down on the big round kitchen table, and they sat next to each other to share.

"Look elsewhere," she said. "Then you can find a nice man, instead."

Unbidden, the guitarist in the Market came vividly to mind, three-dimensional like a hologram. "Maybe so," Oleg said, hope somehow rising up even as he thought the prospect unlikely. He repeated, "Maybe so."

She smiled, and then they sat silent. He filled his empty stomach with pirozhkis, washed them down with hot, dark Caravan tea.

"It's good you eat, Olejka. Your voice will fade away if you grow any thinner, and then what will we do?"

Oleg grinned as he rose to clear the table. It was a joke he'd heard at least once a week since early adolescence.

That she expected no response was evident as she switched topics without missing a beat. "If you don't have your shopping done for Christmas, come with me to the Market tomorrow."

Oleg heard the word Market and his pulse suddenly raced, the thought of going to the place where he'd seen the guitarist—and might see him again—sending him into a panic. He stared.

Finally, Lara asked, "What?"

The descending winter sun shot slanted beams through clouds and into the room. Suddenly—clean, with a full belly, in the delicious warmth of the gold-lit kitchen—everything felt different to Oleg. Things seemed... possible. Maybe he *would* see the busker again. Maybe he'd even talk to him. *A new leaf*, he thought.

"Sure," he said, giving his sister a grin. "I'll go to the Market with you, sis. Why the hell not?"

# ~ 3 ~

## CHAPTER THREE

Beck heard that thought, *never see him again*, every time he remembered the singer for the next two days. He got ridiculously sick of the repetition and supremely annoyed that he kept thinking about the guy at all. Once, on Sunday, he let himself get so preoccupied that he forgot where he was and—while plucking out an upbeat rendition of "I'll Be Home for Christmas" for a fair-sized crowd—loudly ordered the mental image, "Get the fuck out of my head!"

One person slipped him a twenty, apparently having compassion for the insane, but everyone else quietly moved away.

*Nice work, Beck,* he told himself, thinking this could be the year he finally had an apartment and then fucked it up, adding one more misery to the shitpile ghosts of Christmas past.

*Can't do that, though. Parcheesi needs me.*

Sadly, the thought of the formerly stray cat who loved and needed him only made him feel worse, and that's when he realized just how lonely he'd truly become. Just how hungry even for smiles and conversation with some-one who knew him, who cared. Just how deep the well of his hunger for the sex, for the kiss, for the touch of a man who loved him. He wondered if maybe he would never have those things again, and that made him feel like the old, bitter man he would certainly age into if that hap-pened.

Maybe that was why, later that day when he saw George, he fooled himself for a little while. His ex-boyfriend was, for once, by himself. He stood nearby, his shapely legs in sexy stockings under an ankle-length fur—hopefully faux—coat, which surely he needed, as his red velvet hot pants were not exactly designed for winter warmth. When Beck finished the medley of carols he was playing, George stepped gracefully closer, close enough for Beck to hear his whisper.

"Hey, big man. I've been missing you. Thought I'd stop while I had a chance and see if maybe I could buy you lunch."

Beck's first reaction was to be pissed. "Big man" was an old joke between them, a moniker George had stuck on him when they'd been threatened by some fellow home-less who happened also to be haters. Beck and George had talked about moving out of the tent city to get away from them—maybe going to a different city for a while. George hadn't wanted to go.

"Don't worry, Beck," he said in a pique, "it's my five-foot ass they'll be wanting to beat."

Without thinking, Beck replied, "Maybe so, but I don't want you to be hurt!"

George had smiled then as if shyly accepting a compliment. "Aw, that's sweet, baby. But, being my big man and all, you can just open up a can of whoop ass on 'em, and we'll both be fine."

Now Beck wanted to tell George he didn't have a right to call him by pet names, that he'd forfeited that right when he'd chosen to walk off with his sugar daddy and leave Beck brokenhearted and still in the streets. But this didn't seem the time or place, and anyway, Beck was no good with words. Instead, he only said, "Don't call me that."

George's look of mock surprise was apparently meant as a tease, because he put a cajoling tone in his voice. "Oh, don't be like that, Beck. We're still friends, right? Come for coffee, at least."

Beck intended to say no, but somehow "okay" came out of his mouth, and within a few minutes he was walking beside George, automatically shortening his long stride to keep pace with the petite man, just as he'd done a thousand times when they were together. *If that's what we ever were.*

George led him to Storyville Coffee on the top floor of the Market, a shop Beck rarely patronized, preferring to drink cheap brewed coffee and keep more of his hard-earned cash. Once there, George ordered coffee for him without asking him what he wanted, which grated on Beck's temper. It had been sweet when his lover always knew just what he would want, but he didn't like it one bit when his *former* lover got it just right. To make it worse, even though Beck said he wasn't hungry, George got a sea salt caramel roll and chocolate cake with fruit.

*Little fucker knows I won't be able to resist. Worse, we'll have to share, because I want them both.* There was nothing like life on the poverty line to make one's mouth water at the scent of gourmet sweets, and of course George knew that. Deciding he might as well enjoy the decadence while he could, he resolved to ignore the company and accept the gift. *Bribe. Whatever.*

Ignoring George wasn't an easy thing, though. Never had been. For maybe five minutes, Beck managed to savor his macchiato—the best he'd ever had—and tiny bites of the sweets, gazing out the window, looking past snow-loaded rooftops to the white-clad hills fading into the colorless afternoon sky. Then George reached out and laid his hand over Beck's.

It felt electric, and Beck hated it. He pulled his hand away to lift his coffee and sip.

"I really do miss you, Beck."

"Bullshit. Why this, George? Why did you want to 'do coffee'?"

George blew out a breath through flared nostrils, a signal Beck remembered, and he knew it meant George was angry.

"You're a big phony, Beck. You know that? You pretend you're done with me. You're too good for me, or something." He dropped his voice to a hoarse whisper and leaned in close enough to blow his breath across Beck's ear. "We both know, approve of my life or not, you'd love to have me wrap my mouth around this fine hard length of cock anytime. Right now, for instance."

Beck had seen it coming. He'd known George would drop a hand into his lap and discover that, yes indeed, George's ultrasexual personal brand turned him on, had him hard right there in the coffee shop at just the thought of those skilled lips sliding over his flesh. He'd known it would happen, but he wasn't quick enough—or determined enough—to stop it. And it had been so long since anyone had touched him that when George gave him a squeeze he damn near came right there.

"Fuck, George," he said, and it came out a strangled whisper.

"If you want, big man."

"Back off!"

George did, but he looked like the cat that flipped the goldfish bowl, and he said, "Offer's on the table."

"What is it with you, George?"

Beck didn't speak loudly, but he let every bit of the anger and resentment he felt occupy his words. George literally flinched, though he recovered quickly, masking the sudden fright with insouciance.

"You and I—we were a thing," Beck said. "I thought we loved each other. But when you hooked up with your prince, you made sure I knew just what a foolish idea that was. And now... just the other day you strolled by all haughty on the arm of your latest... whatever he is—"

"He's my daddy, you might say, Beck—or maybe you'll get it if I say he's my *Christmas Music*. Money in my pocket. Gives me everything I want except one thing. He doesn't give me a really good time, if you know what I mean. So why did I come see you today? It's been too long since I had something tasty."

Beck sat speechless, motionless, every part of him but his treacherous cock wanting to walk the fuck away from this shallow man who'd broken his heart but didn't even seem to have one of his own to break in return. Just when—knowing he'd be sorry—he was about to grab George's manicured hand and lead him to a quiet corner behind the shops, just when his throbbing, anticipating cock was about to win, George spoke up once more and everything changed.

"Besides," he said, "I had a free afternoon, and you ain't doin' anything important—you never are. I thought I'd suck on a pretty cock to pass the time."

And just like that, whatever it was Beck had thought he saw in George was gone for good. He saw through the too-many layers of makeup, the cheap-style expensive clothes, the phony confidence. It was all a façade, and beneath it was unholy December in human form. Nothing real, nothing light there at all. Beck took a deep, releasing breath and shook his head. "Damn, George. I don't know what you *really* want. I don't think you do either. But suddenly I find I'm not even tempted." He stood up, needlessly straightened his clothes, and picked up his mug to down the dregs of the sweetened brew. "Thanks for the coffee," he said, and turned to leave.

Then he turned back, picked up the chocolate cake and took a huge, "big man" bite, and returned the pitiful remains to the plate. Mouth too full to speak, he waved as he walked away, leaving George to figure things out on his own.

He tried to finish out his performing day, but his teased and lonely cock kept distracting him, so he packed up early that afternoon and went home. When he stripped and got in the shower, he intended only to wash away what felt like some kind of contamination, but when he soaped his cock, it responded to the touch with way more than the usual enthusiasm, momentarily stealing his breath.

He stood for a moment letting the hard, hot spray beat against the tender, engorged crown, then wrapped a firm, well-soaped hand around the shaft and began to stroke. He pulled hard and fast, not wanting to savor the ride, just wanting to get there. And honestly, worried the shower would go cold. Stroking, twisting, running his fingers up over the head, letting his other hand dive between his legs to tug and squeeze at his heavy, hardening balls. He kept his eyes open and stared at his own hard prick, unwilling to allow George's lying face to have even an imaginary moment.

His orgasm was building fast, and Beck didn't slow it down. He just wanted to come, to explode—needed to. He stroked harder and faster until he'd come close to reaching his peak, then did what he knew would send him right up and over the goal. One leg propped high against the shower wall, he pushed his long, thick middle finger into his ass and knocked against the slick pad of his prostate. He came instantly and hard, so hard his knees buckled and left him leaning against the shower wall, squeezing the last of the impossible pleasure from the pulsing nerves, panting.

The water cooled, so Beck quickly rinsed and shut off the tap, then stood stock-still, catching his breath and trying to hold on to something that had come to him, something unexpected. In the moment of orgasm, he'd seen a face, but it didn't belong to George.

He wrapped himself in a towel and went to lie down on his bed, pushing Parcheesi away as kindly as he could. He wanted to think. He wanted to remember the face he'd seen at the moment of his climax. He'd only seen it once in real life, briefly, and he hadn't realized he'd registered it so completely. The gold-flecked brown eyes, thick mop of dark chestnut hair, the white scar across the corner of his mouth that made the red of his lips seem darker and riper.

The face of the man who sang like an angel.

Beck marveled at his mind's revelation, but though he supposed imagining lovers might be fun at times—or at least entertaining—right now it felt devastating. To Beck's dismay, tears clouded his vision.

*What the hell is wrong with me?*

He finally had a life, a home, food, work, music... but a brief, imaginary appearance by a splendid man he'd likely never come to know had reduced him to tears, to hopeless desiring, pointless wondering. Seemingly unquenchable longing. Unwilling to let this torturous state of mind claim another minute, he rolled over and, as most who've slept on the streets can do, forced himself to sleep.

But a haunting voice, a song, played through Beck's dreams.

*"Snow was falling, snow on snow...."*

Beck woke an hour later, just as dusk soaked the snow-banks in purple-tinged gray. He donned his warm coat, gloves, and two pairs of thick wool socks to pad his all-purpose high-tops, then he descended into the streets with no plan except to walk. His feet chose the direction, turning him down Madison toward familiar places. The ice-crusted sidewalks demanded his attention, something that became obvious when a young woman just ahead of him slipped and ended up on hands and knees. She was having a hell of a time getting up, but she wasn't hurt. Her laughter was sweet, and as Beck steadied her so she could rise, he found himself smiling in return.

They walked more or less side by side for the next two blocks without saying a word, but when they got to Six-teenth she waved and their paths separated. It wasn't until Beck had walked another solitary block that he noticed he still wore traces of the smile, and from there it was only a tiny leap to the realization that it had been a long while since he simply shared an honest smile with another human. It felt strange... good.

He continued to pick his way along Madison until he heard music coming from somewhere nearby. He looked up and found that without thinking he'd walked to one of the places he had frequently camped when he was on the streets—before the tent cities, before George. The music—unmistakably harpsichord and strings—came from Trinity Episcopal, the church that billed itself as Seattle's most inclusive. Maybe that was true, maybe it wasn't, but Beck had never been inside.

Not that the building didn't exert its draw on him, but Beck knew he had no place in a Christian congregation. He'd discovered at age fifteen that he didn't believe in anything resembling God. Though his mother's death had been the catalyst for his arrival at that conclusion, it wasn't because of any bitterness. On the contrary, his mother's peace in her last days, the comfort the hospice chaplain had brought her, the smile she wore in the moments before she died as Mozart's "Ave Maria" wove its prayer around her, these things almost made him believe. But his practical mind argued—had always argued—that these things were human. A touch, a voice, music, all the products of human hearts and hands. Beck didn't believe in God, but at the time of his mother's dying, he had decided he believed in people.

In the hard years since, the first part hadn't changed, but the second part had. His belief in people—in families, in love, in compassion and succor—had begun to unravel the day his stepfather, citing Beck's refusal to bow to a Christ he couldn't believe in, had put him out of his home three months after his mother passed. Beck doubted even then that the reason given was the real one—probably it had more to do with his stepfather's fall into a whiskey bottle. But regardless of the underpinning of John's failure to care about his stepson, it showed Beck a side of humanity he hadn't seen firsthand before, struck the first hard blow against his faith in people.

Now, Beck believed in old crows and cats and the joy of hot water from the tap.

And Beck believed in beauty.

Beck believed in music.

The jewel-colored glass in the windows of Trinity Episcopal shone brightly into the wintry night, warm images of saints and well-loved children. Looking at them, Beck could almost believe that their promises, the oaths rendered in lead and colored glass were real. Reliable. True.

*You know better, Beck.*

*Yes.* But the vivid red doors, said to symbolize welcome, would not be locked. He wondered, if he were to enter, would it be like walking into the beauty advertised by the glow from the windows? Would the music filling the space engulf him, hold him suspended in sound?

It seemed a crazy thought. *Probably, I'm just hungry.* It was true, he hadn't eaten anything all day except the bites of cake and caramel roll George had bought that afternoon. He did feel a bit thin. But then, he'd been hungry before. And he'd passed down this street before, even slept outside this very church. Hell, he'd even listened to beautiful music streaming out from inside, more than once. But something was different here and now.

When voices joined the instruments, soared over them, he understood.

Within the sound he clearly heard the man with the angel's voice.

How could he be so sure? Or rather—being honest with himself—how had he known even *before* he heard the voices?

Beck took a deep breath, drawing resolve from the cold night, and climbed the steps to do what he plainly must do—open the red door and go in.

He kept his eyes down as he entered, ridiculously afraid their green shine would alert someone to his presence. When he came even with the rearmost pew, he slipped in as silently as he could and sat down. The only light in the back of the sanctuary flowed dimly from the front where the musicians and singers rehearsed. They went through the piece—something medieval, Beck thought, though he didn't recognize it—a few bars at a time, making mistakes and jokes in equal measure as rehearsing musicians do. Then, after a few words from the woman conducting from the viola, the musicians settled into quiet. Flowing uninterrupted through the entire piece, these musicians united in a way possible only for those who have made music together for a long time.

Beck remembered when he had made music like that with his mother and sister. It struck him then—the singers in this group were a family. He raised his gaze and confirmed that truth, obvious in the similarly thick, unruly heads of dark chestnut waves, the wide cheekbones and golden almond eyes that spoke of eastern European roots. When they finished the piece this time, the rehearsal clearly ended.

Someone—the church, perhaps—had supplied refreshments. As Beck rose to leave, the smell of spiced apple cider assailed him, a reminder of his childhood, the good years before his father died, before the cancer started to win its long battle against his mother's liver, before his stepfather had sent him—literally—out into the hard night with a twenty-dollar bill and the clothes on his back.

The warmth, the reflected crystal glow of the windows, the celestial voice—it was all too much, and before Beck could take three steps he found for the second time that day his eyes burning with tears. Tears. Something he thought he'd left behind with his broken belief in love.

A woman's voice and a hand on his shoulder stopped him. "Hello," she said. "Won't you join us for a cookie? I, for one, find I play better if I have an audience, so I'm glad you were here."

Most of Beck wanted to run for the door, or at the very least politely refuse and stroll away. But he turned to meet the woman's eyes, and they held, on the one hand, simple kindness, and on the other, an echo of the man he'd spent a few minutes fantasizing that very afternoon. Undecided, he glanced at the small group at the front of the room, and locked gazes with that very man—who was smiling at him.

As if he was iron and the man with the gorgeous voice a magnet, all of the various parts of Beck aligned to carry him forward until he was merely a couple of yards away from a young man who, he now realized, might be the most genuinely beautiful human being he'd ever met. He stared until he realized he was doing it, then tried to find someplace else to rest his gaze. The woman who had come to invite him into the group rescued him, placing a paper cup half-filled with warm, aromatic cider in his hand.

"Thank you," Beck said, remembering how to be human. "It smells wonderful."

"From a package"—she smiled—"but I don't mind. My

name's Larishka." She spoke with a slight accent, likely the lilt of an eastern European language like Russian.

"Beck," he answered. "Beck Justice."

"What a wonderful name!" It was the angel-voiced man who spoke, smiling.

Beck felt himself blush hot. It might have been embarrassment, as he had no idea what a person was supposed to say when someone complimented their name. After all, he had no part in choosing it. His trouble might also have been due to general social discomfort—he'd had little practice with casual conversation in recent years. And then, it might also have been the effect of the young man's exquisite, surprisingly low-pitched speaking voice. It... affected Beck.

*Damn. I could listen to this man all day every day, singing or speaking, and never get tired of it.*

"I've never known anybody with the last name Justice."

Reminded that words had been directed at him—not just a lovely sound—Beck brought himself back to the mundane world. "Uh, yeah," he managed, "I suppose it's not common."

"I'm Oleg. All these people are my family. Lara you've already met—she's my oldest sister and the world's most mothering of all hens."

Larishka shot him a look but stayed apart from Beck and Oleg, which was also true of the rest of the group, Beck now noticed. It was as if they'd deliberately left a bubble for the two of them to talk.

"That's Alex, Lina, and Vic." He pointed to them one at a time and elicited a smile and nod from each before they turned back to their conversation. "The woodwinds is my father, Andrei, the violin my brother Pete. My middle sister Kati is over there putting her cello away, and the guy at the harpsichord looking impatient is Bill, Lina's husband."

"No mom?" As soon as it was out, Beck wondered what evil spirit possessed him to say it.

For just an instant, Oleg's eyes went dark and secret, but then he shook his head and said simply, "No. My mother passed away last year."

"I'm so sorry!" Beck shook his head almost violently. "I don't know what I was thinking, asking that... like that. I should know better—my mom, too. Not last year but.... Please forgive me." He finally stopped his mouth, the finish falling out lamely, and took a deep breath. Then he added more calmly, "Really, I am sorry about your mother, your loss."

"Please don't worry. It's fine—was a natural thing to ask."

"Oleg," Andrei said from across the room. "Help with the instruments? We're ready to go."

"Be right there, Papa," Oleg said, then turned to Beck. "So, I know you. You're the guitar man. You play beautifully. I hope I didn't cause you any problems, there, when I started singing. I love that song—the 'falling snow on snow' part. So simple, spare. Elegant, I guess you'd say, compared to most Christmas songs. But I didn't really think about it before I started in singing."

"No, no problems," Beck said, letting his surprise show. "Of course not. You sang so beautifully. It was... perfect."

"Not perfect, but I admit the echo in those hallways at

the Market can make the most of a voice. Listen, we'll be performing tomorrow, so we all need to get a good night's sleep tonight. I've got to go. But will you come tomorrow for the music? Seven o'clock—here. Then, maybe we could go for dinner. I never eat much before the performance, so I'll be hungry." His grin seemed positively playful.

*It's as if he really means it.* Beck found it hard to believe, and even as badly as he wanted every minute he could steal to be near Oleg, he hesitated. "Well...."

"Please, I'd really like a chance to get to know you a little. At least have coffee with me, or a drink." He stopped and looked down toward his feet, biting the side of his lower lip.

*If I didn't know better, I'd think he was embarrassed.*

"Look, I think you're... attractive. Right?" Oleg met Beck's gaze again, having come out with this confession. "And I don't meet many men—no, strike that. I haven't met *any* men who seemed to have the music in them, to love it like I do. We might have some things in common, I think."

At a loss for anything comparably intelligent to say, Beck swallowed. "Yes," he finally said.

"You'll come tomorrow?"

"Yes." This time he said it easier, with an honest smile. "Yes, I will, Oleg. Thanks for inviting me."

"Awesome! You can't even guess how much I'm looking forward to it!"

Oleg smiled to himself as he stood behind a screen of shoppers who'd stopped to listen to Beck. Just moments before, they'd been singing along to "Rudolph the Red-

Nosed Reindeer," but now the small crowd had gone quiet as Beck, faintly smiling, his eyes secret under lowered lids, played bittersweet variations on "Blessed Be the Maid Marie."

Enjoying Beck's minute changes of expression as he responded to the flow of nuance in his music, Oleg was happy to see some joy appear from time to time in his expression. The last time he'd seen Beck play—when he'd shown him to Lara during their outing three days ago—he'd clearly been unhappy, and that had dampened Oleg's pleasure as he watched him play from a strategically hidden spot in the crowd.

That time, he'd known Lara watched him as much as she watched Beck, and as they walked away she'd given him a knowing, big-sister smile that made Oleg blush—something he rarely did. She'd laughed, evidently delighted with that result, but she hadn't teased or questioned him, and for that, Oleg was grateful. But truthfully, the guitarist's rather fierce frown that day had cast new doubt as to the wisdom of Oleg's continuing fantasy that something might develop between them.

Then, as if drawn by some mysterious gravity, Beck had shown up at the family's rehearsal, and Lara had done what she had always done so well, subtly leading Oleg to act as she hoped. The magic of it lent Oleg unfamiliar confidence.

*And so I'll see him tonight.* The thought sent a wave of warmth through Oleg, unlike the anticipation he usually felt when he thought of a man who, say, he'd been cruising on a Saturday night. He wondered if that meant he was a late bloomer—maybe at twenty-two he was finally shrugging out of some pupal adolescence.

As Beck ended the long piece with a two measure *ritardando*, Oleg argued with himself about whether he should go up and say something to him, let him know how much he was looking forward to seeing him later on. He decided against it, afraid he might be reading too much into their meeting, setting himself up for a big fall.

*Better to at least reserve a little dignity.*

He'd half turned to slip away when he saw George—a flamingly out beauty Oleg had met and then avoided in the bars. The man swished his way forward out of the crowd while Beck was down on one knee putting his guitar in the case. When George came to a stop, his red velour hot pants were about a foot away from Beck's face. He said something, and Beck stood, turned, and smiled at George. Oleg struggled to read Beck's expression; there was something he couldn't quite recognize. It gave him pause, but when he saw George throw his arms open in what surely was invitation, Oleg decided the mystery in Beck's smile bespoke some kind of intimacy. Why it should bother him to see it, he didn't know, but he turned away and once again fled the market in a hurry to get away from his thoughts about Beck Justice.

# ~ 4 ~

## CHAPTER FOUR

Beck's December seemed to have taken an upturn. People had become more generous over the last few days—he wasn't getting rich busking at the Market by any measure, but at least he knew his bills were paid and he, Parcheesi, and King Coal would have enough to eat for the next while. What's more, those who stopped to hear him play had suddenly developed a modicum of taste, and they stayed, quietly appreciative, when he broke free of holiday standards and ventured into something different. And the cream on top? *I have a... date. Yes, I think I'll call it a date. With a very fine man who sings a very fine song.*

Added together, all of that improved his mood to the point where even catching sight of George in his small crowd of listeners couldn't fuck it up—even though Beck knew without a single doubt that his asshole ex-boyfriend would have something shitty to say. Sure enough, as soon as the song ended, George came strolling up in his red hot pants and platform-soled boots—which Beck was pretty sure he wore so he could fool himself into thinking he was a bigger person than he seemed. Problem was, George could have been seven feet tall and it would have made no difference. At some point—like when he decided a moneyman was better than a loving man—George had made a wrong turn in life. Every fake layer he'd put on since had made him less like the person Beck knew he could have been and more of a small-minded, small-hearted man.

George had hurt Beck, and Beck didn't like who his former friend had become. But it made Beck more sad than angry—at least most of the time. This particular day, he felt good enough about his own life, he could cut George some slack. Simple solution: the brush-off.

George didn't stop in his approach until he was about a foot closer than Beck would have liked, but—interestingly—his proximity didn't have its usual *remember-the-sex* effect. George spoke in what he probably thought was a sexy whisper, but that fell flat too.

"Hey, Beck," he said, and gave his hips a tiny waggle. "How'd you get over that hard-on you had for me the other day? Prob'ly went home and jerked off thinking about me, right?"

Beck would have been pissed if he thought anybody else could hear, but the crowd had dispersed when they saw Beck lift his guitar strap off his shoulder, an obvious sign he was taking a break. As it was, George's approach made him want to laugh in his face. He didn't—he was feeling charitable—but he did smile at the irony of how close, yet far, George's speculation was from the truth.

"Not exactly, George," he said. Then, before George could think of some other snark to ruin Beck's day, he asked, "What do you want?"

George threw his shoulders back, arms wide as if putting himself on offer. "That's obvious, ain't it? I want whatever you want."

Beck shook his head. *Sad*, he thought, thinking again of how far this George was from the young man Beck once fell in love with. "George, listen to me. What I want is for you to walk away, and not bother me again."

George's face turned as red as his hot pants, and he shoved a fist down on his jutted hip. "You fucker—"

But Beck could be intimidating when he wanted to be, and now he whirled around to face the smaller man, not angry but not willing to put up with any more of the shit George was dealing these days. "Pay attention! Walk away from me now. Don't. Fucking. Bother. Me. Again." He waited a moment while George stared openmouthed, possibly trying to decide if he dared defy Beck's order. "Now!" Beck added, and George fled.

Surprisingly, the encounter didn't dampen Beck's mood, most likely because for once in his not-so-lucky life, even though it was still dark, dreary December, he had something to look forward to. And he'd done well tips-wise, so he could pack up early, which is exactly what he did.

As he left the protected warmth of the Market, he noticed a sharper than usual chill in the late afternoon wind. For a fleeting second, it troubled his good mood, but he shook it off. What was a little weather? He had a date....

"Beck."

The quiet call came as he was passing by a line of homeless people huddled against the wall of a shelter, undoubtedly hoping to get a spot inside once it opened for the night. The voice seemed familiar, but Beck couldn't place it right away, and for a moment he couldn't find a face it might belong to. Then... *Fuck!*

Not able to think of any other way to address the man he hadn't seen since he was kicked out of his home and onto the streets eight years ago, Beck said, "Dad?"

"Yeah."

Taking a step closer, Beck took in his stepfather's condition. It looked as though the alcohol he'd taken refuge in after the death of his wife—Beck's mom—had eaten away his once formidable angry strength.

*I can't feel sorry for him. No. I can't afford to feel sorry for him. He deserves this.*

*Doesn't he?*

*But even if he does....*

"Fuck," he said. "Dad." It was a pronouncement, not a question or the beginning of a statement. The two words were all he had to say on the subject, at least for the moment. He looked away, down the street at wool scarves and coat hems flapping in the wind. He took the cold air deep into his lungs, let its chill invade his spirit. Maybe, he admitted, his luck was not as good as he thought today. It was, after all, December. What did he expect?

He tried for a moment to argue against what he knew he had to do.

*He'll get into the shelter. He'll be all right. He just needs to get out of the cold. He doesn't want to change anything anyway, not really. I know how drunks like him are. Once they're on the skids, that's it.*

He knew all those things were true, or at least more probable than not. But, with a sigh, he admitted it made no difference.

"Come on," he said. "Can you walk okay? I'll take you home."

Beck soon found out his stepdad, former Army captain John Gillette, was in rough shape. Not just alcoholic, destitute, and homeless, but sick. He'd managed about a single block, Beck guiding him by the elbow, when he doubled over, trying to keep his feet against an unbelievably forceful cough.

Beck's good mood had so totally disintegrated that he wanted to mete out the same kind of heartlessness John Gillette had once shown him. He wanted to just keep walking and then, maybe, if the guy could keep up, he'd let him crash on his tiny balcony or send him upstairs to the roof with one of his blankets. He could keep King Coal company.

By the time he faced the truth that no way was he built for such cruel behavior, John had managed to straighten up most of the way. Though he was breathing hard and wobbling, he managed to lock onto Beck's gaze with a look of such pitiful pleading that Beck almost found compassion. He didn't quite make it that far, but he did find conscience. He simply wasn't capable of dealing a death blow to another human being, hated or not, and he knew without an ounce of doubt that if he left this man out in this night's December freeze, it would kill him. Still, he kept thinking of Oleg, and he wanted to salvage his night if he could.

He had time, he thought, if he hurried. He could take John to the apartment and feed him—maybe toss him into a hot shower. Put him to bed.

*Hell, he can have my bed.*

*Reality check. He'll probably piss in it.*

*I don't care, as long as I don't miss my date!*

*He should be in a hospital.*

*It will take forever to get him checked in!*

*I'll just leave him at the door.*

But in the time when Beck lived on the streets, he'd been around the block with sick drunks. He knew that if John could walk at all, he would leave the hospital the minute Beck was out of sight. Beck couldn't do it. But he could, and he did, argue himself out of taking him to the hospital, convincing himself that being warm, out of the weather, hydrated, and fed—if he could eat—would shore up John's reserves. He'd be okay while Beck went to hear Oleg sing and share coffee with him afterward. And... dare he think about a kiss, a single soft kiss on those dark, shapely lips?

So Beck herded and supported and half carried John back to the tiny apartment on Twenty-Third and loaded him into the elevator, resenting every minute but unable to make himself sufficiently uncaring to dump the guy. Once inside, he heated water and made John drink some—he felt pretty certain tea would nauseate the man, but he thought getting warm from the inside out might help. Seated in front of the heater vent, John rallied enough to focus and speak.

"Thank you."

Not sure *you're welcome* would be honest, Beck didn't answer.

"You hate me," John ventured.

"Yes," Beck said, helping him doff his filthy, stiff clothes and shoes.

John said, "I know," and that effectively ended the conversation.

It worked out well that the shower had barely enough room to pivot in a circle, and the bathroom itself offered not much more space. Beck was able to lean John up against the wall and hold him with one hand while urgently soaping him down, bracing his own back against the bathroom wall. He got wet, but that was easy enough to cure, and once he threw John's clothes outside to the far corner of the balcony deck, the result was Beck could breathe without choking on stink. The process depleted what little strength John had found, though, and Beck learned that dressing a grown man who was completely unable to help with the process posed quite a challenge. He was sweating and winded by the time he got sweatpants, T-shirt, and socks on the man and wrapped him in both wool blankets.

He checked the time. Five after seven. Oleg's performance was scheduled for seven, so he would certainly miss that, but Beck thought that if he hurried, he had time to force some instant soup into his stepfather, change his clothes, and dash over to Trinity Episcopal in time to catch Oleg before he left. He could explain....

*No, I'm not telling him about John.* If he told him his homeless, drunk, sick stepfather was sleeping in his tiny two hundred square foot apartment, he'd no doubt have to tell him more of the story. He wasn't ready to do that. What would Oleg, a young man with a big, obviously close family think of Beck's sad history?

*At least give me a chance to let him know me a bit before I scare him away.* Beck had no idea who the hell he was asking, but he felt slightly better for having asked anyway, so he added an out-loud "Please."

His plan fell apart when, just as Beck was setting water within reach of John's hands, ready in case he awoke while Beck was gone, John began to retch.

"Here, Dad," Beck said, thrusting an empty margarine tub under the older man's mouth to catch whatever meager stomach contents would come up. But then, "*Fuck.*" Because what came up was a lot of bright red liquid surrounding dark, thick stuff like coffee grounds. It wasn't hard to figure out what was happening. Stunned and scared, Beck sat for probably five seconds that each took a thousand years to pass, unable to move. Then he repeated the refrain, "Fuck," hopped up, grabbed his phone, and dialed 911.

Oleg had to smile at Lara—she was trying so hard to make him feel better.

"Hurry, Olejka! It's ten after eight."

The performance had ended with the most heart-wrenching "C'est vous en qui j'ay esperance" he'd ever sung, and on time for once, at seven fifty. He'd tried to lag, greeting attendees and packing up, hoping despite Beck's absence he would show at the last minute, would have some good explanation that didn't involve anything like

George. But his family bustled him along with them as they hurried, hungry and wanting to get to the Dumpling Tzar for pelmeni, as they never ate dinner before a performance.

As for Lara, it clearly hadn't escaped her attention that Oleg felt like sitting down for a good cry. "You need vatrushka! And maybe cookies. You sang your heart out, tonight."

And of course Oleg went along with the family. What else would he do? He might *feel* like crying, but he'd never cried over a man yet, and he wasn't about to start. Strangely, he regretted that Beck missed the performance almost as much as losing the chance to have coffee with him afterward. Although he admitted he'd looked forward to sitting across a tiny table and watching the man's eyes. Beck had memorable eyes in Oleg's opinion, a soft and mutable-seeming green.

Nevertheless, Oleg decided to put thoughts of the guitarist out of his mind. It was obvious what had happened—he'd hooked up with George and forgotten all about the drab little Russian singer. So Oleg would forget about Beck, and he had a plan for doing just that.

*Sweets with the family, fine. But then I'm going out.*

*What a dull Friday night*, Oleg thought. *Not a single hot fuck in the entire place—at least none that are my type.*

He sipped at a vodka martini, finding its taste as uninteresting as the male pickings at the bar. The place was the third boring bar he'd been to so far that night, and the drink he was working on the fourth of its lackluster kind. He was trying to drink it slowly. He usually didn't drink so much, because he was usually busy with other things, so now his brain felt a bit foggy.

Probably, that's why it took a few minutes for him to realize that George was there at the bar, busy out on the dance floor sliding up and down the well-dressed but sweaty body of some older and clearly richer guy who didn't even remotely resemble Beck Justice.

*Hmm.*

Oleg began trying to piece together how long he'd been sitting at the bar and whether George and his fella had been there the whole time. When the waiter went by, he asked for some water, hoping it could wash out some of the fuzz from his brain and he could clarify his thinking on the subject.

When the waiter thumped the glass down on his table as he passed—clearly not happy with the prospects for a tip from a guy drinking water—Oleg picked it up and downed it. And yes, it helped. With his mind focused, he could clearly see the truth: it didn't change a thing.

Regardless of where George was now, he might very well have been with Beck during the time Beck was supposed to be meeting Oleg—that had been hours ago.

*Besides, he blew me off. What difference does it make whether the reason involves hot-pants George?*

Still, Oleg just couldn't get interested in his customary chase that night. He plopped a large tip on the table, grabbed his coat, and went home. Just before he fell asleep that night, he had a disturbing thought.

*What if something bad happened to him?*

Oleg wasn't much of a God-believer. His family—except

his Jewish-born father—were faithfully Russian Orthodox, and sometimes Oleg went with them to St. Nicholas Cathedral, but he wasn't one of the faithful and didn't feel any lack because of that. Nevertheless, he let whatever powers may be know that if something bad had happened to Beck, he hoped it wasn't *too* bad. And if some sort of unfortunate event were the case, he, Oleg, was sorry for thinking the worst of Beck.

*But most likely*, he concluded, *the man is just a colossal ass.*

The night had been long and horrible, and in the gray morning Beck felt nearly dead on his feet. He'd left the hospital just before the sun finally, belatedly as always in December, began to provide more light than the streetlamps, but to his mind the illumination remained too dim, a far cry from anything that should be called *daylight*.

How had he been fooled into thinking December could ever be anything but a cruel cosmic joke? So many problems now bumped shoulders in his crowded head, he didn't even have room to remember his optimism of the previous day. It seemed, for one thing, he was going to be saddled with his stepfather. Not only did he want never to have anything to do with John, he didn't have anywhere to put him! They couldn't both live in his ridiculously small apartment. He wasn't sure the management would even *allow* a second tenant. He wouldn't be able to even feed him reliably. What if his tips slowed down, or if he lost his spot on the list of Market buskers, or if he got sick and couldn't play? Speaking of which, was he even going to manage staying on his feet to play music that very day?

As far as that last question, he truly had no choice.

He had no other income, and aside from the possibility of food banks and food assistance, he felt fairly certain he couldn't get help from the government or anyone else. That thought reminded him that ex-Captain Gillette had once had some sort of pension. He had been found, for reasons unknown to Beck, to be a disabled veteran.

*I wonder if it's bad juju to hate a disabled vet.* This was a new line of thinking, and something Beck was too tired to pursue, but it did dawn on him that whatever had happened to John, whatever made him disabled, might also be what made him an asshole. At least in part.

*I'll have to think that through later.*

He arrived at the apartment, fed Parcheesi, ate some oatmeal, and hit the shower. He almost collapsed straight into the bed, but stopped when he saw the bloodstains all over everything. Sure that he was an evil person for being pissed at John for bleeding on his only bed linens and blankets, he gathered everything, threw it in the shower enclosure, and soaked it with cold water, hoping for the best. He scrubbed at the stains in the mattress until they were mostly gone and covered them with towels. Then, unable to maintain any longer, he set his alarm for two hours and collapsed onto the dry portion of his bed, dressed in boxers and socks, with three cotton flannel shirts, his coat, and the worn-thin throw rug that usually decorated the floor draped over him for covers.

At the sound of the alarm, he woke from a dream of the singer.

*Oleg.* He couldn't believe that his thoughts had strayed so far into misery that, while he was at the hospital with

John and even afterward, he didn't once think about Oleg and the missed date. *Oleg.* He wondered if there was any way the sweet-seeming man would ever believe he hadn't blown him off on purpose. He'd *wanted* to get in touch, to tell him he couldn't make it, though he hadn't wanted to give the despicable state of his existence as excuse. While he was at the hospital, though, things were just crazy—John with ruptured varices in his esophagus, almost dying, Beck remembering being there in the same hospital, waiting just the same way, as his mother was dying. It was hell both times.

When the emergency had more or less passed, the hospital staff made demands on Beck, determined to extract information about John Gillette that Beck just didn't have—had never had. So he'd had no time to think of other things, not even Oleg.

And, bottom line, he couldn't have contacted Oleg anyway. He had no idea how to get in touch with the man. All he knew was that he possessed a celestial voice and had an engagement to sing at Trinity Episcopal at a time that had already passed before Beck had a moment's peace to think about it.

*Thank you very much, December.*

Still feeling sluggish, he caught a bus to Harborview. He felt obligated to check in on his stepdad, as ridiculous as that seemed on the surface. If there had been anybody else in the whole world, he would have left it to them, but the only other family Beck knew of was his sister, Della, and she'd moved across the country, severing ties to keep John from coming near her or her children even before the asshole kicked Beck out of the house. He didn't think there was much hope she'd come back to take John in—or even give him the time of day—just because he'd drunk himself nearly to death.

John's eyes were shut against the glare of the bright light over his bed, but apparently he wasn't sleeping, because when Beck walked in, he spoke to him immediately. "You're here."

"Yeah."

"Nowhere else to be?"

"Fuck you."

"Yeah. I know."

"Do you? Do you really get what it's like for me having to—"

John's seizure, probably DTs breaking through as the protective Librium thinned in his blood, made it impossible for Beck to finish the diatribe he'd launched into. Later, when he left the hospital, he admitted that was probably a good thing. For Beck to spew hate all over John wouldn't help his chances, and it wouldn't make the world a better place.

He'd already talked himself into accepting responsibility for his stepfather. Now he had to talk himself out of hating him. If he held on to the venom, it would keep them both sick.

He shivered on his way to the Market until he tried deep breathing and found that it warmed him despite the cold air filling his lungs. Probably, the shivers were more from exhaustion than cold. When he walked inside, he decided it was a little early yet for him to set up, and he made a snap decision to go to Storyville, splurge on coffee and a waffle before getting started. He'd forget about everything and enjoy a well-earned treat.

That was his plan, but when he actually had the fragrant beverage set before him, all he could do was sit and stare out the window at fog and dirty snow and wonder over and over about three things: whether he'd ever find a way to forget Oleg Abramov; the way December had stolen his chance to know the singer; and how it could hurt so very much.

*It's him.*

*He doesn't look so good.*

Oleg headed for the order bar at Storyville, pretty sure Beck hadn't spotted him when he walked in searching for caffeine to medicate his hangover, which he figured was no more than he deserved.

*It's what I get for drinking most of the night instead of hooking up or, better yet, just going home to sleep.*

Not that he would feel any better this morning if he *had* found someone to go home with—in truth he never felt that great after one of his "nights out." It was more like a chore—system cleaning, so to speak. He would go out, get screwed, and then for a while not only did he not need to do it again, but he didn't want to, because in reality it wasn't any fun. It only made him hungrier for what he knew damn well he couldn't find with any bar pickup. He knew it actually did work for some people—he'd been to weddings of very happy men who'd met in a bar. It just wouldn't happen for him. Maybe because he didn't expect it. Maybe because all he knew how to do in a bar was cruise for a hookup.

Honestly, he didn't know how to look for what he truly wanted anywhere. It had been some kind of miracle that he'd been so comfortable talking to Beck after the rehearsal the other night. Probably, he had to thank Larishka for paving the way for him. Plus, he'd been in that centered, focused state of mind that nearly always resulted after he immersed himself in music.

At the bars, it was more tunnel vision than focus. He might have thought of finding someone special before he started the evening prowl, but in the midst of it he only looked ahead as far as getting laid. Oddly, a drink or two usually just made that more true. The excursion last night was the first time his search for sex yielded zip. So in addition to hungover, he felt frustrated.

On the other hand, he might not have fared much better if he'd gone straight home after the rehearsal, because when eventually he did seek out his own pillow, he couldn't sleep for wondering about Beck.

Yes, caffeine was definitely top priority today. He had no classes—it was winter break at Cornish—but he had shopping to do, an activity he generally loathed but didn't mind so much when he was out to find holiday gifts for his family. That, in fact, was his favorite part of the holiday season. He'd hoped caffeine would keep him awake enough to enjoy it. It still might, but seeing Beck had already cast a negative pall over the morning.

*He really doesn't look well.*

"Triple shot macchiato, grande," he told the young

man behind the counter. "And I guess a waffle. Two waffles—I'm hungry. And fruit."

After he paid he looked out among the tables and saw Beck looking at him. The man wore an expression Oleg found difficult to read, but he thought there was a hint of *pleading* in it. He wasn't sure, though, if Beck was pleading for him to stay away, or pleading for him to come sit at his table. He also wasn't sure he wanted to go sit with Beck, even if he *was* silently asking.

He tried a small experimental nod in Beck's direction and received widened eyes, a tentative smile, and a decidedly agreeable nod in return. Concluding Beck did indeed want Oleg to share his table, Oleg started in that direction, even though he still felt both angry at Beck for not showing up last night, and betrayed by his own foolish heart for having pinned ridiculous hopes to Beck's shapely chest.

*But today, really, he looks a little... run-down.*

Maybe something bad truly *had* happened to the guitarist last night.

*If so... well, here I am going to his table, so it looks like I'm giving him a chance to explain.*

"Hey," Beck said. "Oleg. I'm, uh... glad I ran into you."

A white-aproned server brought Oleg his coffee and interjected, "Both you guys' waffles will be up in a minute. We had a little problem with the machinery and got a little behind. Sorry."

Oleg nodded and smiled absently, but his attention hadn't wavered from Beck. Not only did his eyes have the red, heavy look that comes with lack of sleep, but he hadn't shaved, and he looked hastily clothed and combed—not quite pulled together. Oleg thought back to the other times he'd seen Beck, confirming in his own mind that though his clothing was obviously low budget, he'd always looked carefully groomed.

*Yes, something's happened. So let's just find out what it was.* "Hello, Beck. You know, I was really looking forward to seeing you after my performance last night."

"I know! I'm sorry!" Beck nodded vigorously, the words almost exploding out of him, as if he'd been holding them in and thinking he'd never get a chance to say them. And he kept nodding, and repeated the apology twice more.

Finally Oleg interrupted him. "So what happened?"

Beck's features moved through a number of expressions, some light, some seeming pained, until finally settling on what looked to Oleg like a kind of resigned sorrow.

"It's just... something came up." He didn't look up at Oleg then, but his Adam's apple moved up and down as he swallowed a few times, so it was apparent he was going to try to say more.

Oleg waited, took a drink of his macchiato. It was perfect and damn strong. That was at least *one* mark on the plus side for the morning.

Beck lifted his gaze to settle on Oleg's. "I had to take care of... something. It was unexpected." After they sat silent for a moment, gazes unwavering, he repeated. "It was unexpected."

Oleg wanted to interrogate further, but realized he didn't have a right to do so. He had a sense that the truth, whatever had really happened, was something Beck wished *wasn't* true. It seemed to be causing him some anguish, and obviously he didn't want to talk about it. Oleg's heart reached out to Beck, searching, and found something to hold on to in the man's eyes. Right then Oleg knew two things. One, he was going to take a chance on getting to know this man. And two, hope had already regained its footing in the slippery landscape of his emotions.

*Which means*, he warned himself, *I could get really hurt.*

# ~ 5 ~

## CHAPTER FIVE

Something—he didn't know what—drew Beck's attention away from the dreary scene outside Storyville's windows. He glanced around and immediately spotted Oleg at the order counter. His heartstrings strummed a snappy little rhythm with joy until he stopped to think. Odds were astronomically against the gentle, gracefully attractive man wanting to talk to Beck ever again, even just to give him the time of day.

He was grief-stricken at the thought, though he could scarcely credit such a thing. How could he grieve losing someone he never had, never knew? Still, he'd learned what grief felt like, and this was it.

*Fuck you, John Gillette*, he thought, and though he knew he didn't quite mean it—it just wasn't in him to be that coldhearted—he really, really *wanted* to mean it. He wanted things to be different—for last night never to have happened, for another crack at it—wanted it so hard it burned inside. Yet, at the same time, he wondered how the *hell* just getting the chance to get to know the guy could mean so much to him. He'd never been a believer in love at first sight, or soul mates, or reuniting with people from a past life. Not that he'd ever actively disbelieved these ideas—they just didn't compel his belief, or even his attention.

But now he stared at Oleg Abramov and thought, *You never know.* But if he and Oleg had somehow been fated to meet, that just made the present circumstance worse. Except...

*He's looking back at me!*

Beck's first response was *Damn, what do I do?* Then he contemplated the look on Oleg's face—he seemed maybe irritated, but also uncertain. With no more thought, Beck gave a tiny nod and a barely there smile, daring to hope Oleg would come and share his table. As Oleg started walking toward him, Beck's nerves went on high alert. This might be his chance to put things right and start again with the object of his desire. He didn't want to muck it up.

Beck waved vaguely at the bench opposite him in the booth. Oleg sat down, and suddenly the world changed for Beck. The tabletops were shinier, the light outside sunnier, the clink of dishes and flatware more musical. Feeling light as air, Beck took in the aromas of cinnamon, espresso, lemon, and yeast, but they were unimportant, dim in comparison to the bright, glowing scent that belonged to Oleg. A little sweat, a little sex, a little lavender. Maybe a little booze. Extraordinary.

The bubble of delight encompassing Beck popped when Oleg said, "You know, I was really looking forward to seeing you...."

*Fuck.*

Beck had no idea what to say, where to begin, or how much he should reveal. He knew, *knew*, without question, Oleg's family had nothing in it like John Gillette. If Beck started explaining, he'd come out of it smelling like a loser.

*Because I am.*

*No!*

But affirming his self-worth wasn't enough to allow him to risk revealing his family affairs. He stumbled through a vague apology, fully expecting Oleg to either grill him or take his coffee to whichever table was farthest from Beck. The waiter zipped up in an obvious rush, dropped waffles in front of each of them, two for Oleg and one for him, and moved on, leaving the air at the table strangely disturbed in Beck's perception. And somehow, all the sounds around them then added up to a deep, aching silence.

Until Oleg smiled and spoke, his few words every bit as captivating as his songs. "Well, it's water under the bridge, right? I'm starving." He began to eat with beautiful gusto, swallowing coffee to wash it down after every few bites. He didn't speak again until his second waffle had been whittled down to a single square. "So, I never saw you around here before the other day. How long have you been playing music at the Market?"

Even the crap he had to put up with at the hospital that night wasn't enough to destroy Beck's better than average spirits. All the while he was talking to the financial office and the social worker and the VA liaison, he clung to the happy, impossible thought that Oleg seemed to like him—despite his secrecy about his stepdad. Despite his awkward social skills. Despite his scruffy face, untrimmed hair, raggedy clothes, and secondhand guitar.

*He really does. He seems to like me.*

It had been evident as they laughed through a second coffee, Beck having successfully argued with himself that the price of the latte was high for coffee but rock-bottom low for an excuse to spend more time with Oleg. And it had been evident when Oleg talked to him, told him about his family coming from Russia, and how his sister Lara had been so overprotective of him she made him hide instead of going to kindergarten for three days until their mother got a call from the school and the secret was out.

Beck had laughed at that too, but he had remembered how, before Della left, she had also been protective, trying to make Beck hide from John after their mother died and John fell in love with Jack Daniel's. He almost slipped and told Oleg about that, because Oleg was so easy—easy on the eyes, but also easy to talk to. But he stopped himself, and the two of them fell into a silence that turned comfortable after only minutes. Oleg, on his way out of the Market, walked with Beck to where he was setting up for the first hour and stopped to listen. When Beck began to warm up with a simple, very old Christmas tune called "Rug Muire Mac do Dhia," Oleg surprised him by knowing—and singing—the Irish words.

Not many people had been around yet to hear, but the tune had a cheerful lilt to it and Oleg styled it well, so those few who were there had applauded before walking away. The two men stood near each other for a few minutes in the deserted, dim lit hallway.

Nervous, Beck said, "I always thought that was a strange concept, God making Mary pregnant, like that song says. Hardly seems fair to the poor girl."

Oleg had looked at him with surprise on his face, and then burst out laughing. "Yes," he said. "Yes it is—quite strange."

Then he lifted his face to Beck's and kissed him, short, soft, sweet, right on the lips.

So when Beck helped get John's VA medical coverage restarted, and when he made arrangements for John, now that he was going to be sober, to get on the wait list for the VA Domiciliary, and when he reluctantly agreed that, until a bed opened up there, John could live with him (hopefully without incurring the manager's wrath) so he'd have an address for his disability benefits, he stayed in a pretty damn good mood.

Once he had John as squared away as a man in his condition could be, he got four solid, refreshing hours of sleep. He even woke up smiling at fleeting memories of dreams full of good things—Oleg singing while colored lights danced, Oleg's lips touching his and lingering, and a strangely accurate reliving of a moment from a December long past, when child Beck helped his mother cut star-shaped cookies.

Parcheesi glared at him when he tried to encourage a game of "catch the mousie," and King Coal seemed a little wary too. The scruffy old bird refused to come near the food Beck brought out for him until Beck stopped whistling.

*Which means… I was whistling.*

*Even though the calendar says I'm still trapped in the wastelands of December.*

*What the hell?*

Beck shook his head at the weird feeling of smiling while freezing his ass off on a winter rooftop to feed an indignant crow, all the while unsure how the hell he'd find room to sleep in his own apartment for the next who knows how long because he'd be housing the man who, of everyone he'd ever known, *least* deserved his compassion. Ridiculous. Awful. Funny. He laughed. And he realized for the first time in his life that compassion didn't hinge on whether one *deserved* it. Because, for him at least, *having* compassion meant he could live with the mirror's reflection.

*In December?*

*Especially in December.*

At the Market that morning, Beck found himself smiling at the strangest things. A toddler with an elf-ear headband, which kept sliding down over his eyes so that he bumped constantly into the woman leading him by the hand. A sweating off-duty Santa Claus with a black five o'clock shadow, red jacket unbuttoned to reveal a T-shirt showing Hello Kitty in a Santa suit holding a Hello Kitty doll in a Santa suit. Beck didn't worry much about the music, either. He played old lute music and J. S. Bach, and people smiled and tipped him anyway.

He got requests! Surprised, he took them.

"Can we sing Jingle Bells?" screamed a kid—boy or girl, Beck wasn't sure—about six years old.

Beck couldn't help but smile, wondering if the child was that enthusiastic all the time, and also wondering whether he'd ever been quite that excited about life. He decided that maybe he had. When an image of Oleg popped into his mind, he all but shivered at the remembered touch of his lips. He thought, *Maybe I could be again.*

"Well," he said, "what if you and your friends"—a passel of screamers, in fact—"sing it, and I'll play it on the guitar." Predictably, the entire bunch loved the idea, and Beck played the simplest chords he'd played for any reason in years. When their singing, or more properly shouting, died away and they were gone down the hall, Beck felt as though the song had been his best ever masterwork.

He smiled. A lot.

And though he didn't smile very much when he picked his stepdad up from the hospital to take him home that afternoon, he did thank the young woman who wheeled John out to the medical transportation car twice, once for her help, and once for her "Merry Christmas." He even added, "You too!"

He gave John his bed, made a run to Value Village to pick up thick quilts, more blankets, more sweats and T-shirts and socks so both he and John could be reasonably clothed at the same time. With the quilts on the floor that night, he slept just fine. In the morning, chores and grooming done, he left John with a stack of military thrillers he'd also picked up at the thrift store.

"You didn't have to do that," John said.

"I know." Beck felt himself edging away from his ready-to-smile self, hearing John's morose and maybe self-pitying tone. He took a deep breath and tried to step back into his better mood. "Listen, Dad. I saw them, they were cheap, and I remembered that's what you used to read, back before.... So I got them. Consider them an early Christmas present, if you like."

John merely nodded, no change in his expression, but he took a book from the top of the stack as Beck left for the Market.

The hour was early, and Storyville felt warm and... *kitcheny*, Beck decided, and not too crowded yet with workers looking for a buzz before starting the daily grind. Beck waited in his window booth, watching the door for the moment Oleg would come in. They hadn't seen each other the previous day at all, and Beck had known they wouldn't.

Oleg had sounded almost apologetic as he explained, "I'm going to have to go out to Ravenna and a couple other places, and I told Lina I'd work with her on a new piece we're supposed to sing New Year's Eve."

Beck had said it was okay even though he wished it weren't the case. "I'm going to be busy too," he'd said, which was absolutely true.

Even though the day without Oleg had gone by swiftly and well, as he waited now at Storyville, Beck felt an un-familiar, pleasant anticipation, as if tiny happy horses in-side him waited with sleigh bells tinkling to take Beck and his romance for a ride. Unbidden, a frightening thought arose. What if he doesn't show? What if something happened? Or what if he wants to get back at me for not showing up that first night? Or what if...?

George Harrison's "While My Guitar Gently Weeps" began to play, but it took Beck a minute to remember that meant his phone was ringing—it happened so rarely. He froze for a long second, sure it was Oleg saying he wouldn't be there. Then he remembered he'd not yet given Oleg his number, but John had it in the flip phone the social worker at the hospital had given him.

"Beck," John said, once the line was open.

"What's up, Dad? You okay?"

"I'm uh... I'll just get out of your way. You've been great. More than I deserve. But, you know... I'll be okay."

Beck stared at the tabletop, digesting his stepdad's words until their meaning clicked. "No!" He fairly shouted the word, then glanced around. A few people looked his way, so he leaned forward on his elbow to hide his face in his hand and tried to keep his voice low. But his emotions exploded: worry for the fate of the gnarly old drunk he called Dad if he hit the streets; frustration at the difficulty involved in reasoning with a newly sober alcoholic; most of all, anger. All he had done in the past few days, all the red tape, the hoops he'd jumped through.... He'd given up his routine, his privacy, even his peace of mind, and damn near blew his chance at happiness, and he felt furious to realize John remained the asshole he'd always been, having not an ounce of gratitude.

So when he spoke into the phone, maybe his voice wasn't really as quiet as he hoped. Maybe everyone could hear. Beck didn't really care. "Listen, you *stay* there. Don't leave! Don't fucking leave. I'll come home now and we can talk about it."

Having gotten John's reluctant agreement, Beck slapped a tip down on his table and left, glaring at all the nosy onlookers.

But then he saw Oleg among them, looking shocked and bitter.

"Don't leave? You'll be home to talk about it?" Oleg asked, but it was clear he'd drawn his own conclusions, and he didn't wait for an answer. After shooting Beck a disgusted frown, he shook his head, waved dismissively, and walked out of Storyville.

"Wait," Beck said, but it was weak, and Oleg was gone, and he might as well not have said it at all. He hated John all the more in that moment because he had to choose between trying to salvage his attempt to rescue his stepfather from death on the streets, and trying to catch Oleg and plead with him to understand. The first could be life or death; the latter was probably futile.

Knowing he could make better time walking than on the bus, he slung his guitar over his shoulder and set out for home, stretching his long legs into a brisk stride. He had no idea what he'd do when he got there. Part of him wanted to toss John out in the cold merely to be done with it, mostly because John had cost him any chance he might have had with Oleg.

*But that's not really true, is it, Beck?*

*I'm not going to go there!*

*Face the truth. Why did that door of opportunity slam shut?*

*Oleg wouldn't have understood!*

And there it was: the truth. *He'd* blown his chances with Oleg because he hadn't trusted him to have the same compassion he'd recently discovered in himself. Oleg had talked about his family—about coming from Russia, about his Jewish-born father and the mother who'd given up everything for him, about the sisters and brothers that kept him ensconced in love, affirming though sometimes mildly suffocating. Yet Beck kept his home, his past, and his stepfather secret, afraid to let Oleg know the real him. Afraid Oleg would judge. Would dismiss him.

Or far worse, *pity* him.

As if a man whose soul held such beauty, whose single kiss could shine away December's shroud, could then possibly have so little substance.

As Beck started up the steps to his apartment, overwhelmingly sad but calmer now that he'd let responsibility fall on his shoulders where it belonged, he was more determined than ever to take care of his stepdad despite John's attempt to escape life. Before he turned his attention to that task, a last regretful thought of Oleg came to mind. *God, I didn't even give him my phone number.*

*But... yesterday he gave me his!*

Beck stopped in the middle of the third flight of stairs and pulled out his phone. He wasn't much on using it for anything but a clock and to play a few free games—he had no one to call, generally, and he'd never sent a single text. Now he studied his options. Texting, he decided, would be a better idea than calling. If he called, Oleg might just hang up and block his number—Beck was pretty sure such a thing could be done. But if he texted, he'd at least read it first. He had to concentrate to figure out how, but he managed at last.

*"Please read this. I know what it sounded like, but it wasn't what you think. Come to my house, right now if you can, and you'll see. Please, Oleg!"* He added his address and, since he wasn't sure if his number would show up, added that. When he hit Send, he felt tight with apprehension, but he also noticed hope flitting around the corners of his visual field like summer butterflies.

Something about Beck made Oleg hungry in a whole new way. Not that he wasn't sexy as hell. Long legs, long fingers, long, slender neck. By the time they'd spent two hours together, Oleg entertained visions of lingering nights spent heating up a cool bed with the man, and the kisses they'd shared—countable on the fingers of one hand—definitely piqued his appetite. But he also craved something else with Beck, something extra. Like the "special sauce" on a burger. He wanted to lie up against him *after* sex—maybe even instead of sex, someday, just feeling his warmth and his callused guitarist's fingertips scraping over his skin. They could have been doing anything together, Oleg decided—talking, watching movies, whatever. It wouldn't have mattered as long as a goodly portion of their skins were in contact.

Oleg's mother had done her best to instill in her children a belief in the miracle of love at first sight. It had happened for her. She'd been a rising star at the Moscow Conservatory of Music when she'd seen his father perform at a wedding. They'd become devoted to each other within days, married within months, and through all their years—and despite all she'd let go of for a poor Jewish boy—she'd never once regretted her choice.

Oleg supposed it *could* happen to anyone, and although he hadn't quite arrived at confessions of love, he had begun to think it *might* have happened to him.

Which was why it hurt so bad, hearing Beck on the phone begging *someone*, a someone he'd never confessed to having, not to leave him.

## ~ 6 ~

## CHAPTER SIX

The scene at the apartment didn't turn ugly until after Oleg arrived. Before that, Beck had turned the heat up, made himself and John both instant coffee, straightened up the bed, and sat John down at the tiny table, pulling up a mop bucket for his own seat.

"Listen," he'd tried to reason. "I know things seem impossible now, because you just got sober. It's hard."

"You don't know."

John stared into his coffee but didn't drink it. Parcheesi apparently thought table time meant food, or else he liked the old man, because he was rubbing up against his legs and purring. John reached down absentmindedly to scratch behind the cat's ears, the tenderness in the gesture thoroughly surprising Beck.

"Right, I don't—I've never been addicted. But I do know what it's like when things feel impossible, and they *can* get better! Give it time!" The mostly one-sided conversation had continued, Beck assuring John that he didn't mind having him there for a while, that John would be out soon enough when his ship—in the form of VA benefits—came in.

When Beck mentioned the VA, John said, "I hated Iraq. I'd never seen anything like it, never even thought I'd get shipped out. Army three years—Germany and Japan. No fighting. Reserves ten years—never expected the call."

Beck sat silent, never having known a single thing about John's military service. He didn't know if he wanted to know more, but even if he did, he didn't think questions were a good idea. John seemed balanced on some point between living in the present and reliving something even worse in the past. But John took a long pull from his cup, gave it a strange look as though surprised to remember it wasn't booze, then kept talking.

"I was scared, but I killed people anyway. Soldiers, civilians. A woman. I remember all the time. Your mother, she made it so I could forget sometimes." He got up and headed for the bathroom.

At first Beck worried he'd do something crazy in there—his razor was right out in the open. But tiny apartments dismiss the notion of privacy, so Beck knew John was only taking a piss.

When he returned to the table, Beck said, "Dad, you need to stay here awhile."

"It's too small. You don't have room." And then he got up and shambled toward the door.

"Damn it, Dad!"

They both jumped at the sound of the buzzer from the com. To Beck's great relief, the voice on the other end of the com was Oleg.

After buzzing him in, he turned back to his stepdad. "Sit back down. You need to stay."

John tried to push past him, and Beck stood in his way. When Oleg knocked, he opened the door while trying to block John from access to it.

He didn't even have a chance to greet Oleg before he was practically shouting again, "Just sit down, damn it!" Resisting the urge to be rough, Beck took his stepfather's elbow and guided him back to the table.

In the quiet moment that followed, Beck introduced Oleg to his stepfather and briefly summed up the events of the last few days.

"So that's where you were the night you were supposed to meet me at Trinity."

"Yes," Beck said. "This morning, on the phone—"

"There's no room for me here, son," John interjected.

All the tight knots Beck had used to keep himself together snapped, and he spat, "You don't get to call me son! You kicked me out into the streets when I was fifteen and never looked back! I never was your son to begin with, and you made it clear I never would be." He took a deep breath, glanced helplessly and hopelessly at Oleg—what must he think of him now? More quietly, he said, "I don't want you to go, Dad. I want you to get your life back. But never, *never*, call me 'son' again."

John just looked at him blankly. After a time he repeated, "There's no room for me here."

"It's okay," Beck said, but he'd just about run out of the steam he needed to continue fighting this uphill battle. He went to the long window and stared out, amazed that he'd ever thought the bleak gray of December had faltered. "I don't mind," he said. "Really."

He heard Oleg and John speaking very quietly behind him, but he let his interest slip away, feeling tired. Maybe the four hours' sleep he'd had each of the last two nights hadn't been enough. When Oleg came up and stood beside him, he sighed, but he didn't turn to look.

Oleg rested his hand on Beck's shoulder. "I had an idea. I talked to him. He'll do it."

Beck felt nothing at the news except confusion. "What are you talking about?"

"He'll stay here if he doesn't think he's crowding you."

"I told him it was okay!" A fountain of frustration welled up in him and came out as tears. *Great. This will do wonders for Oleg's opinion of me.* "Fuck!" He lifted an arm to angrily swipe at the tears, but Oleg caught it and, apparently stronger than he looked, used it to pull him around to face him. For a fractured second, Beck looked into Oleg's gilded dark eyes, and then he found himself wrapped up in the man's arms, his head cradled in the crook of Oleg's neck.

*Lavender, sex, and sweat.*

For each of the last several days, three o'clock in the afternoon had brought Seattle a brilliant sunbreak, rays streaking across the city streets, striking gold from puddles and dirty piles of remnant snow. This afternoon, the moment came while Oleg and Beck were on the bus on the way to his Greenwood home.

As the sun bathed Beck's face, he gripped Oleg's hand as if he feared drowning in the light. No trace of tears remained, but Beck remained unsettled. Wherever their bodies touched, Oleg could feel the nervousness coursing through Beck like a shaky aura. And he kept talking, saying the same things in different ways.

"He'll leave."

Oleg tried not to sigh in exasperation. "He said he'd stay as long as you had someplace comfortable to be. I promise, my place is comfortable." He'd told Beck earlier about the deal he'd worked out with John—that if the older man stayed at Beck's, the young man could stay with Oleg. He had almost, but not quite, lied to Beck about where he lived.

Beck had asked, "You live by yourself?"

"Yeah. I have an over-the-garage apartment. Like what they call a mother-in-law suite." But Oleg's answer hadn't included the fact that the garage belonged to his family's house.

Now, on the bus, Beck said for the third time, "He won't feed Parcheesi."

Oleg refrained from saying again that Parcheesi was a weird name for a cat, and went straight to the refrain. "He likes the cat. He promised."

Beck surprised him then, bringing up a different subject. "I'm sorry," he said, seeming quite sincere. "I should have told you about my family before, when we talked."

Oleg turned from staring straight ahead, tilting his head to meet the taller man's direct gaze. He smiled, reflecting on how happy he'd been to discover he'd been wrong about the meaning of the phone conversation he'd overheard that morning, to learn what a deeply kind person he was, this man who'd been occupying his thoughts and fantasies for days. He wasn't sure he understood why Beck hadn't wanted to tell him about John, but heavens knew, it didn't matter. "You are so totally forgiven," he said, smiling.

Beck rewarded him with one of his dazzling grins in return, so Oleg leaned forward and planted a kiss—more than a peck but not by much—on his luscious lips.

When they got to his place, he marched Beck straight past the big house, knowing and not really caring that at least one sister would be looking out a window and would see. He closed the door behind him, and instantly all the welcoming, here's-the-tour, make-yourself-at-home speech he'd planned was simply gone. The man, Beck, this tall, sexy male who was lovely inside and out, stood right there, mere feet from the bed Oleg had fantasized him into several times over. And all that compelling hunger that had been building inside of him—yes, for sex, but also for *extra*—clamored for his attention.

"Beck," he said, breathless.

Thanks and praise to every Russian deity and saint, Beck understood. All the tension left his tall, trim body, and when Oleg slipped a hand under his open jacket to pull him close, Beck's entire being seemed to hum with desire. Oleg couldn't be sure, but he convinced himself in that moment that the other man's desire was like what he felt—that Beck wanted *him* more than he wanted sex.

Beck moved first, stepping close and pushing long fingers through Oleg's hair, grasping it firmly and pulling it back to tilt Oleg's face up. Kissing him, Beck slid his lips over Oleg's willing mouth, sucking and nipping, pushing in with his tongue, keeping it going for long moments until his breathing came hard and fast. He stopped, crushing Oleg against him and gulping air.

"Oleg, damn! I want you!"

To Oleg's ears, the words straddled the line between a demand and a plea—and when their eyes met, he saw uncertainty among the heat. All of it made Oleg want Beck more, and he answered by holding Beck's gaze while grinding his hips against Beck's thigh. The hard evidence of Oleg's arousal—his want—couldn't be missed, and he soon saw the light in Beck's eyes change with recognition. Then the man's gaze burned into his, and they slipped and slid together into pure abandon.

They stripped and scattered their clothes about in the hurricane wind of their lust for each other. Oleg landed on the bed naked, hard, and pleasantly pinned by Beck's weight, and then Beck started kissing him again. For an unknowable length of time, Oleg felt like all he was, all they were together, was made of sliding lips and sucked tongues, licked ears and love bites. As Beck rolled a little to one side, he gazed down at Oleg with a knowing expression—although Oleg wasn't sure what that meant.

Beck licked his lips, gathered breath, and said, "You are so much more than beautiful, Oleg Abramov."

Oleg groaned in sudden heat, shocked and reeling. No one had ever said his name during sex before. He'd had no idea it could change things so much.

Beck raised his hand to squeeze and flick over one of Oleg's nipples, using his mouth on the other—biting and teasing and sensitizing the nub until Oleg could hardly stand the touch, could hardly stand the thought of being without it. Impatient, Oleg slid his hand along the narrow path of hair that started just below Beck's navel, and when he reached Beck's firm cock, took him in hand. Beck's erection—long, straight, strong, flawless—looked and felt just as Oleg had imagined it would. His hand slick with precum, Oleg stroked, loving the smooth hardness of it, rejoicing in his lover's sweet moans.

*My lover.*

Oleg was unused to the term, and it struck him like ringing a cathedral bell. Every part of him shivered at the combined sensation of such a thought, his hands on Beck, and Beck's mouth and hands on him.

"Oh," he said, and Beck groaned in response. "Oh," he said again, and added Beck's name. It tasted sweet in his mouth, whetting his appetite. He moved swiftly, pushing Beck away and down onto his back to give himself access to Beck's beautifully unique, steel-strong, wet erection. He leaned over, took the tight crown into his yearning lips, then slid down the length of Beck's cock, opening his throat to draw in the last inch. With his lips nested in the hair at the base of the shaft, he massaged and sucked rhythmically with his tongue and throat.

Beck's belly muscles tightened, and in a rush of air, he said, "Oh fuck!"

Oleg took that for approval, feeling his own cock jump and twitch at the rush of heightened desire that coursed through him from knowing he was giving true pleasure to his lover. *My lover,* he thought again. *My lover, Beck.* He continued with the treatment he was giving Beck's dick until he thought of Beck's hands—his beautiful hands, how they glided and teased over the guitar strings, coaxing just the right sounds.

*God, I want those hands.* He rose up and moved his mouth to Beck's fingers, sucked and licked for a short minute, then slid his body up until his own cock touched Beck's left hand. Beck did something Oleg didn't quite have words for, sweeping fingers up over his cock and—rather than grabbing at it—gathering him in. He lost himself completely in the sensations of Beck's *lovemaking*, shocked as hell to find himself thinking that word, but with no interest in analyzing it at the moment. Beck used his hand on Oleg's cock, his fingers long enough to stretch the length of it and include Oleg's balls—which had begun to sweetly ache. Oleg wanted more, was planning to beg for it if he had to, but first he wanted to savor Beck's touch. Strong fingers, pulling, stroking. Smooth fingernails, rough calluses, Beck's fingertips playing over Oleg's cock and balls.

When Beck moved his hand to the tender perineum behind Oleg's testes, Oleg opened wide, gratified when Beck followed up by continuing the next caress down to his ass. The muscles around Oleg's hole convulsed at Beck's touch, and then loosened as Beck massaged. Oleg had so little awareness of anything else at the moment, that he was surprised when he felt Beck's tongue lap at the precum pouring from his slit. The sensation overpowered him, and he said something wordless but loud.

Beck laughed, a low, sweet, sexy chuckle that made

Oleg's cock jump even though Beck had moved both hand and mouth away.

Beck asked, "Shall I make you come now?"

The words almost did just that, but he shook his head. "Fuck me, Beck?"

The groan that came from Beck then burned itself into Oleg's mind, a sound so sweet and hot, Oleg knew he'd never forget it, would crave it over and over, possibly for the rest of his life.

He said, "Wait," and rolled off the bed. He'd never had any man in his rooms before, never taken a man to his own bed, so, regrettably, no condoms and no lube were stashed nearby. He hadn't thought about it until just that moment.

He came back from the bathroom with the goods in hand and held them out.

Beck said, "Thank God. Or somebody," and by the time Oleg was back on the bed, he'd sheathed his cock. Beck made a sweet game of lubing Oleg's ass, taking his time around the perimeter, teasingly ducking in, stretching and massaging. It was another first for Oleg. He hadn't known any man would ever do sex the way Beck was doing it, taking his time. He damn near wanted to tear up over the thought of everything he'd been missing, but he was too busy digging the way it felt.

"Ready?" Beck asked, then kissed Oleg's lips before he could answer.

Oleg nodded into the kiss, said, "Mmmm."

"You sure?"

Again Beck covered Oleg's mouth with his, and Oleg couldn't answer aloud.

"I can't fuck you," Beck finally said, "until you say yes."

This time Oleg saw his opening and almost shouted, "Yes! Beck, please." *Please?* Where, Oleg wondered, did that come from? He never had to say please to get someone to fuck him.

"Oleg, you *damn* sure don't have to say please. Because, the truth is, I've never needed anything, anyone, like I need you now." With that, Beck pushed his cock against Oleg's opening.

The burn felt sweet to Oleg as Beck just kept pushing in one steady slide until he was all the way in, filling Oleg perfectly and making him too anxious for what was yet to come.

Oleg was glad that the time for pillow talk was apparently over. Beck wrapped his arms around him and brought his mouth down to Oleg's for a long kiss, sucking and releasing and setting up a rhythm for his thrusting hips.

The beat was slow. Strong. Unrelenting. *Fucking perfect!*

Tension and heat climbed steadily, and then all at once, Oleg crested the rise into a climax unlike any he'd ever experienced—or maybe endured was a better word. It went on and on with aftershocks as Beck drove into him, faster and harder now. Breathless and senseless, he came back to full awareness just as Beck's rhythm broke. Holding him impossibly tight, Beck said Oleg's name, low, slow, and *sostenuto*. As Beck's orgasm subsided, he kissed Oleg again,

so hard and deep this time Oleg thought he might lose
himself in Beck forever.

~ 7 ~

## CHAPTER SEVEN

Beck hadn't had a man for quite some time, but he didn't think that explained the way Oleg pulled at his mind and body before they made love. And he didn't think it explained the way Oleg's pleasure made Beck feel like he'd found some special purpose in life, above and beyond anything mundane. And he was certain it didn't explain the way he'd wanted to cry out *Oleg, I love you* after he came, which had led to a hard and deep—maybe profound—final kiss. He'd undertaken it to keep himself from speaking the words, but he thought they'd possibly made themselves known anyway. Regardless, the kiss he buried them in seared him down to his soul.

*Soul.* If there was such a thing. If he kept the idea separate from any concept like *God*, he felt inclined, now that he knew Oleg, to believe that yes, *soul* might be a thing. But if that were so, did that mean he and Oleg might be *soul mates*? Beck decided not to go there yet, but thought he might entertain the notion further at some future time.

He'd just realized his musings probably meant he was going to fall asleep when his stomach growled, loud and rude. Oleg laughed—also loud and rude, but sweet nevertheless. The growl recalled to Beck's mind the fact that he hadn't eaten anything since oatmeal at dark thirty that morning.

"You're hungry," Oleg said.

Beck only smiled.

"Me too. We should eat."

Beck realized then he hadn't seen a kitchen in Oleg's apartment. No microwave, no refrigerator. Not even a hot plate.

He must have looked puzzled, because Oleg said, "Yeah, no kitchen." After a minute he continued. "Listen, remember how I forgave you for not telling me about John and stuff?"

"Mm."

"Well, maybe you can forgive me for not telling you the whole truth about my living arrangements."

Beck raised his eyebrows but said nothing.

"You know that big house up front? It's my family's. That's where the kitchen is."

Beck nodded, then said, "Okay," but he put a question mark on the end of it, because it seemed like there might be more that Oleg wanted to say.

"Only my dad and Lara really live there now—well, and Vic, but he's a merchant sailor, and when he's in port, he tends to land in jail so he's not around much. But Lina and Bill live next door, and Kati and her family have the house that butts up against the back of this lot, on the next street over."

"You all stay pretty close," Beck said, because he felt

as though something was required. Then he got up and headed the few steps to the bathroom for a piss and a quick rinse—lube remains had started to get sticky—and to toss the condom.

Oleg raised his voice to be heard over the sounds Beck made in the bathroom. "And Alex and Pete live in the duplex across the street—they each have half."

Beck came out of the bathroom, nodding to show he'd heard. He wanted to kiss Oleg some more, but the man just kept talking, so he decided to get dressed.

"We're like our own mini-Moscow, here."

Beck stared, because what could one say?

"Do you forgive me?"

At the exasperated sound of Oleg's question, Beck realized he'd been waiting for absolution all along.

Stopping with his pants halfway up his thighs, he offered the needed assurance. "Oh! Yeah. Yes, of course. What's to forgive?"

Oleg took a deep breath and without further ado moved on to the next thing on his mind, which seemed to operate along his own peculiar logic. "So, if we're hungry, and we want to eat, that's the kitchen we go to—in the house."

"Okay." Beck said, shoving his jeans back down and kicking them off. "Can I borrow your shower, then, so I won't smell like sex? I'll be quick so we can go get food."

"Wow, you have a one-track mind when you're hungry."

Beck laughed. "Not really, Oleg. I'm thinking about you.

I just need food to keep my strength up before I get back to that."

Oleg smiled a rather coy smile. "I'll shower with you. Faster, right?"

It wasn't, though, as being naked and slippery proved a distraction. But the hot water—though longer lasting than at Beck's apartment, did run out eventually, encouraging them to get out and get dressed.

Beck had little faith in his own social skills, and the weather outside reminded him it was still December, and his very good mood began to retreat as he followed Oleg into the back door of the family home. Larishka, however, was having none of his hesitant company manners and soon seated him—almost forcefully—at the round table next to Oleg. A plate of sandwiches landed in front of him a short time later with hot, dark tea served in a glass, which was nested in a metal holder with a handle.

"This is the Russian way to drink tea," Lara said, her accent providing a rolled *R* and, Beck thought, almost a trill in there somewhere. "*Podstakannik.*" She touched the metal holder to indicate her meaning.

Beck's mouth was full, which meant he could get away with a nod. He did, and then quickly followed with another bite. The sandwiches were ham with some kind of pickle and very good, and he didn't mind at all that Lara babbled on. The sun had set some time ago, and the kitchen was lit by a Tiffany-style fixture overhead, the yellow and red glass blossoms limning Oleg's chestnut hair and lashes in gold. Beck ate, but he watched his lover eat too, and he thought it a wonderful sight.

Until he remembered John sitting alone in the little apartment. Beck had showed his stepfather his stores of food—canned soups and sandwich goods and even frozen pizzas—before he left, and made sure he knew how to operate everything. But that didn't mean John was eating, or even keeping the place warm.

Suddenly uneasy, he swallowed and said, "Hey, Oleg? Do you mind if I run back and grab my phone? I think I should call and make sure John is okay."

Lara apparently thought being Oleg's older sister made her surrogate for that role with Beck too, and she interjected, "No, no. You don't go run out through the rain—or is it snowing again? Use the phone in the living room. Just to your left as you walk into the room."

The room, an old-fashioned haven full of overstuffed things, polished wood, bric-a-brac, and various musical paraphernalia, settled around Beck like a favorite quilt the minute he entered. Even the Christmas tree standing in the corner near the woodstove and the menorah on the mantel felt okay. With the comfort came sadness, because for the first time he admitted that December might not really be blackhearted. It was horrible *for him*. But that was because he was alone, and he hadn't had a good thing happen in December since he was fourteen years old.

But, he realized, he hadn't done much good for anyone else either, during any December since then.

*There's a connection there*, he thought.

John answered his call almost immediately. "Hey, son—sorry, Beck."

He seemed in good cheer, and Beck didn't want to upset that. He also felt a little ashamed of his temper earlier, so he said, "It's okay, Dad. Don't apologize. Are you doing all right? Did you eat? No trouble with the heater?"

John assured him all was well, and then added, "That lady from the social services was here. Wanted to make sure I wasn't being taken advantage of."

It took Beck a number of seconds to realize the sound that followed, though stifled, was laughter.

"I didn't tell her you were gone—said you just went to the store. She's nice enough, I guess." After a moment, he continued. "And someone from AA called. Bob D. Wants to take me to a meeting tomorrow at noon."

"Yeah? What did you tell him?" Beck, surprised that his stepdad seemed talkative, sat down on a love seat and promptly sank deep into the embrace of the Abramovs' cushions. It wasn't unpleasant, but he felt like an imposter.

"I was surprised he wanted to do it—it being Christmas Eve tomorrow and all."

*Fuck! Christmas Eve.* Beck's mind raced. He hadn't even considered the holiday. He'd be hanging out alone in Oleg's room! He was sure the family wouldn't want a stranger in the middle of their traditions—*yes, this kind of family, they've got traditions, capital T.* It would be less painful to be home with Parcheesi. Even with his stepfather.

*Fuck! John will be alone. Newly sober. Short blocks from prime can-you-spare-a-quarter territory.*

John's voice eventually cut into Beck's thoughts. He'd said yes to the meeting. So that was good. But still, as he ended the call with some final words of encouragement, Beck felt worried and defeated all over again.

Back in the kitchen, Oleg sat at the table alone, and Lara was nowhere to be seen. Beck stood, hovering. "Tomorrow's Christmas Eve," he finally said in answer to Oleg's questioning look. "I... I think I shouldn't leave John...."

"Beck, I didn't say anything before, but—"

Lara bustled back into the kitchen and interrupted, apparently not aware or not caring her little brother was already speaking. "And so. How is John?"

Evidently, in the short time Beck had been occupied in the other room, Oleg had told her all about John and their temporary living arrangements. From her tone, it seemed she saw herself as fully involved. Possibly even responsible. Beck assured her John was okay, and that pleased her.

Beck again broached the subject he'd started on with Oleg. "Tomorrow's Christmas Eve—"

That was all he got out before Lara threw her hands in the air and said, "No, no, no. Your stepfather can't be alone on Christmas Eve. You'll tell him to be ready at three, and I'll have Alexi or Peter pick him up. He can stay on the cot in Papa's office, and we'll get him back to your apartment in time to feed the cat on Christmas."

For some reason, Beck said, "Parcheesi."

Apparently, Oleg had told her about even this small detail, for now she said, "The cat. Yes."

Actually it was Lina and Bill who fetched John from the apartment, and when he arrived at the house, where Beck and Oleg were already sunk together into the couch looking at a family photo album, Beck smiled, relating well to the bulldozed and helpless look on his stepdad's face.

Privately, Beck was glad John would be there to receive some of the rampant solicitude. He didn't feel grumpy about it, though, when the family greeted him cheerfully and saw to even his vaguest wants. He didn't think they were being phony. He didn't indulge in self-pity at all. That was a change in Beck, and it didn't escape his notice.

The family did have traditions, ranging from when to have hot chocolate to who passed out gifts and what to sing before dinner, which turned out to be something Russian—no surprise—about a sleigh ride with tingling, freezing fingers. Beck tried to reserve a corner of his December pessimism, but he was warm and fed and the object of many smiles, and he knew he'd never be able to deny the happiness he felt that day. Not even if the twenty-sixth rolled around and turned the month back to black.

He and John even became partners in a game of hearts. They lost, but they laughed. Even if it was all essentially make-believe and would be struck to shards at midnight, the day was too delicious while it lasted to be tasted lightly. So Beck dove in. He laughed, he ate, he even tried to sing. But mostly, he watched Oleg. The man captivated him—all of him. Sure, he was sexy, and Beck savored the few kisses and flirty touches they snuck when no one was near to see, but there was so much more to him. His voice, of course, but also his grace, his quick mind. His smiles—he had a whole repertoire of them, it seemed, and every one of them meant something a little different.

Beck thought he could dedicate a lifetime to the language of Oleg's smiles.

But of course the day ended. The family then tucked itself in—some members in the big house, some in their nearby homes. John had already retired to Andrei's study, and Beck and Oleg walked back to the rooms above the garage. Of course they made love that night. For Beck, the sex that time was a prelude to the romance of sleeping in Oleg's arms.

Early in the morning, they made the delightful discovery that they shared a tendency for morning wood. Further discoveries ensued, and then, more satisfied than he ever remembered being, Beck fell asleep again, cradled by Oleg and a weak but warm beam of transient sunlight. As he started to wake later, he inhaled the indescribably delicious scent of Oleg. But when he reached across the bed, then felt around, then opened his eyes, he found he was alone.

At first he was afraid he'd rudely missed Christmas breakfast—another family tradition—but he'd been told it was set for ten and the clock said nine. He rose and washed and dressed and waited. That made him nervous, and he started thinking, *I should probably leave.*

Just when he'd decided it was time to sneak away, Oleg came in with a thermal pot full of coffee and a package wrapped in dark green satin foil.

"What are you doing?" Oleg set the thermos and package down on his tiny desk and moved to the door, as if sure it needed blocking.

*Damn, it's strange. He reads my mind.*

"I know what you're thinking, Beck, but you can't leave yet. For one thing, John's still here. For another, you're expected for breakfast. Lara sent Vic to the store for Bisquick and had Lina bake the coffee cake recipe off the box because John told her it was your favorite."

"No shit?"

"And besides, please stay, Beck. Because I asked you to. You'll be fine here."

"Yeah," Beck said, sitting down on the too-small stool that appeared to live under Oleg's desk. "I'm fine. I am. But it's still December."

Oleg looked at him, wearing a slight, crooked smile that Beck decided indicated he was worried, puzzled, and somewhat amused. When Beck stayed silent, he said, "I don't know what that means, Beck."

Beck heaved a tired sigh—tired though he'd slept a full, satisfying sleep and woken refreshed—and said, "Neither do I."

Oleg came close and straddled Beck's lap, wrapping his arms around him, laying his head on his shoulder. After a moment, he reached for the package he'd been carrying when he came in, and offered it to Beck.

"It's from Lara," he said, and got to his feet to pour them both coffee.

"What is it?"

Oleg laughed. "The point of the wrapping is so you don't know what it is before you open it. If your boyfriend tells you what it is before you do that, it spoils the surprise. You're acting like you've never got a Christmas present before."

Beck's mind tumbled through possible responses:

*You're my boyfriend?*

*I don't like surprises in December.*

*It has been a very long time since I got the last one.*

In the end he said nothing, just tugged at the ribbon and then, frustrated, tore at the paper.

"Larishka's a photographer," Oleg said helpfully, now that it was clear the thing was a framed photo. "Still uses film and has a darkroom in the house. She's amazing and—"

Smiling at Oleg's nervous rambling, Beck put a stop to it with a kiss. He sat back and smiled, letting Oleg know he didn't need to explain. Then he took a long look at Lara's work. A black and white print, and in it Beck smiled in the instant just before his lips met Oleg's for one of those stolen kisses they thought no one had seen yesterday. Beck looked like someone he didn't recognize, or maybe someone he remembered from a very happy summer. Oleg glowed—figuratively but literally too, the wall sconce behind his head creating a halo that seemed to cast its shine onto Beck. Beck's hand, long fingers looking more graceful and lovely than he ever would have thought, gently cupped Oleg's head. He remembered the moment, of course. He'd been there.

But if these two people had been strangers, Beck would have thought they were in love and had been so for years.

Oleg fidgeted nearby, antsy for some reason. Beck looked a question at him, and he said, "She inscribed the back. Turn it over. I want to find out what she said."

Beck turned the framed image over in his lap and read

aloud, "To Oleg and Beck, to help you see the way you fit together."

It was true, they did fit. That truth almost buried Beck, falling over him like snow, inexorable. He knew it would bury him and either keep him alive through every December or kill him like a stray dog in a hard freeze. Overwhelmed with the danger of possibility, he sat as still as if already frozen.

Then, opening a small, still-warm corner of his mind, he looked at Oleg and saw him smile gently and begin to move, dancing to a tune only he, at first, could hear. But he began to hum, and then to sing—quietly yet roughly, in a voice entirely different from the one with which he sang "In the Bleak Midwinter."

It was a song Beck knew, liked but didn't often hear—Augustana's "We Fit Together." Not Beck's usual fare. Alternative, a little shouty in the recording, but not as Oleg sang it. The perfect song for this particular moment. He didn't know all of the words, but he whispered the ones he did know as Oleg sang, hearing them a new way, an *unlonely* way. About cold so deep it hurts. About the push and pull of gravity and of love. And about the wonder—like in the photograph—the frightening, perfect wonder of finding a beautiful someone. When Oleg finished the last of the lyrics, he stepped in close to Beck, and Beck wrapped his arms around him.

"Lay with me," Oleg whispered, paraphrasing the song's final verse. "Stay by me. We'll be good together, I think."

Still holding on to Oleg with one arm, Beck picked up

the framed photo of their not-secret kiss and turned his head to study it again. Slowly, he smiled. "Oleg," he said, mostly because the name tasted sweet on his tongue. Then, half teasing, he said, "My place is too small for two people—just ask John." Tentatively, feeling brave, he added, "This place too."

Oleg rolled his eyes, an endearing expression Beck hadn't seen before, and one that came with a unique version of his ever-intriguing smile.

"Easily solved, Beck! We can work it out together."

Beck put the picture down so he could wrap Oleg up with both arms. He said, "Hmm," into Oleg's ear and gave the lobe a playful nip. "Is it April already, do you think?"

Oleg drew back to give Beck a thoroughly perplexed, brows-drawn-down-in-confusion look. "What?"

"Do you know," Beck asked, "how much I like watching your face?"

This time Oleg raised his eyebrows but said nothing at all.

Beck laughed. "As good a reason as any, I guess, to give *together* a try. Let's do it."

**Dear Reader,**

I hope you enjoyed reading Falling Snow on Snow as much as I enjoyed creating it! If you found it to be a good read, please consider dropping a quick review where you purchased the book or on Goodreads. Next, enjoy the epic playlist of all the songs mentioned in the story. If you'd like another dose of holiday love, be sure to read on for a sample from *The Holiday Home Hotel*.

# FALLING SNOW ON SNOW EPIC PLAYLIST

## Falling Snow on Snow Epic Playlist

"In the Bleak Midwinter"—the song the whole story pivots around (Lyrics 1872, Christina Rosetti; melody before 1906, Gustav Holz)

### Part I: Holiday standards
*(This is the music Beck Justice, a guitar-playing busker at Pike Place Market, really hates playing—until love lights up his heart.)*

"Jingle bells" (James Lord Pierpont, 1857)

"Rudolph the Red-nosed Reindeer" (Johnny Marks, 1939)

"White Christmas" (Irving Berlin, 1942)

"Up on the Housetop" (Benjamin Hanby, 1864)

"I'll be Home for Christmas" (Kim Gannon, 1943)

"The Dreidel Song" (1927 or earlier, origin disputed)

### Part II: Less Well-known Holiday Songs
*(Beck likes these better. Most of them are "early music." Some of them Oleg sings in his haunting high alto voice.)*

"Blessed Be that Maid Marie" (1902, in its present form)

"Maoz Tzur" (13th Century)

"As I Lay on Yoolis Night" (14th Century)
"Rug Muire Mac do Dhia" (Probably medieval)

## Part III: More Early Music

*(Beck plays these while alone in his apartment before he meets Oleg. He likes that they have nothing to do with holidays.)*

"Sumer is icumin in/The Cuckoo Song" (13th Century)

"Danger Me Hath, Unskylfuly" (Medieval)

"Blowe, Northerne Wynd" (Probably c. 1300 CE)

## Part IV: Blues Rag and Blues Rock

*(Beck loves to play all kinds blues. Some of these he played last summer in Seattle taverns. The last one in the list is his ring tone.)*

"Black Mountain Rag" (Leslie Keith, 1930s)

"Tears in Heaven" (Eric Clapton, 1991)

"Birds" (Neil Young, 1970)

"While My Guitar Gently Weeps" (George Harrison, 1968)

## Part V: You read to the end of the story—you know what these two are all about. (Hint: Love, joy, and family.)

"Russian  (or Ukranian, or Minka's) Sleigh Ride" (Before 1830)

"Fit Together" (Augustana 2014)

# MORE HOLIDAY MAGIC FROM LOU SYLVRE

MORE HOLIDAY MAGIC FROM LOU SYLVRE

## The Holiday Home Hotel

*About the Story:*

Daren Novak and Gunny Schuler have known each other since freshmen days at the University of Washington, where they'd started a romance Daren assumed would last. But at the start of winter break, Gunny bowed to the dictates of his lifelong religion and his overbearing father and left UW never to return.

After a failed marriage, Gunny built a quiet life embracing his gay identity, and left his North Dakota home, his marriage, and his father's business for a forestry and teaching career in Oregon. Meanwhile, Daren has built up his own life around managing a unique holiday venue, the Holiday Home Hotel, and performing for the guests in drag as "Dare."

A decade has passed since they last saw each other, but now winter's harsh weather brings them face to face—helped along by a minor goddess and powerful forest spirit. Too much hurt might lie between them now to fix things, but interfering supernatural beings are determined to force them to try.

(Read on for a sample!)

## Prologue

"Why did you come, Lelia?" the forest spirit asked, short-tempered as always. "Your time isn't here yet. The trees need to dream through their winter sleep, and if I wake them up for anything it'll be shenanigans, not some of your silly-sweet *mercy*."

"Spring is months away, yes, Leshy, but I have other concerns, and don't be so mean. Without my lovely springtime, your trees will dream their winter right up to the end of eternity, won't they? Besides, we're friends, aren't we?" She rolled onto her side, wanting as much contact with the cool green earth as possible and not caring a whit about the mud that would cake in her thick white fur.

Also, she knew Leshy would like the pose and she wasn't beyond taking advantage of the soft spot he harbored for her. "You look good as a bear, by the way. Consider golden fur next time you take this form, though. I love golden fur."

"Don't change the subject." He pushed his long snout against his great, black paw, a gesture of frustration.

Of all the goddesses, Lelia could be the most exasperating—though Leshy admitted he wasn't immune to her energetic charm, and this wily-dog form she'd taken only added to her allure. He closed his eyes and let himself fall to the ground beside her. Glancing up after a satisfying squirm in what was now well-churned mud, he caught sight of the ancient red cedar that often housed his spirit in this place, an ocean and many years from the forest he sprang from, a place he'd sought out as his old forests had met with annihilation. The cedar—his 'old man' tree—was 'empty,' one might say, while he played bear, but still it seemed to send a scowl his way and say, *back to business, you old fool.*

"What concerns, Lelia?"

"Hmm?"

"Pay attention, hound. What 'other concerns' are you on about?"

Lelia jumped up to all fours and snarled at Leshy—in this form only a little bigger than her present shape. "I am no hound! I am a shepherd. Belgian, to be specific."

"A dog's a dog." Leshy grunted, and he was pretty sure Lelia wouldn't realize he was laughing at her.

"And soon a forest spirit is going to be a squashed bear, if he keeps it up, because this dog's a god."

"Goddess, minor."

"Less minor than a Leshy."

"What concerns?"

"Luck, of course. And love—"

"Love is your mother Lada's territory."

"And I'm my mother's daughter. Besides, when a human I'm fond of is miserable without love and won't do anything about it, then mercy is needed, and I'm all about mercy." She sat down, and wagged her bushy tail through the leaf mold, very satisfied with that argument.

"Is mischief involved?"

"Absolutely."

"I'm in, big sister. What do you need me to do?"

"Bring snow, Leshy. Lots and lots of it." She stopped to sniff the breeze and detected just a touch of the particular human scent she was waiting for. "Yes. Right about now, I think."

# Chapter One

*Glacier View Wilderness, Washington State, Present Day*

Sometimes, when Gunny walked through a forest, the trees whispered to him. Not secrets about the lives or spirits of trees; holding an advanced degree in forestry, he already knew the facts, and although one couldn't know for sure, he'd never put much store in Green Man legends. The secrets the forest told were Gunny's own—echoes of best friends, lost moments, years-old joys and regrets. This particular December day, layers of cloth and leather buffered the cold, the murmur of snowfall muted Gunny's thoughts, and the trees, it seemed, whispered louder than ever.

And, wouldn't you know it, with all that going on, Gunny got distracted. Instead of thinking about how the trail was disappearing under snow, how the lumpy shapes covered in white were less and less distinguishable, how the lowering sky sent wind sluicing under the limbs of tall evergreens and stole whatever stubborn heat remained in the air, he thought about Cher. Or, not about Cher exactly, but about one of her famous songs.

Specifically, he was thinking about "If I Could Turn Back Time," because he wished he could. Because the words were exactly right. And because one night years ago Daren had dressed up in Cher drag and sang it for him.

*Daren. Damn I miss you. Still, really. And I wish—*

*University of Washington, Seattle, 2001*

Gunny started his first year at the University of Washington with stomach butterflies so large and lively they shook his medium-sized but sturdy frame. He'd been warned by his father, and the pastor of his Seventh Day Adventist church, and just about everyone he knew, that evil would tempt him at every turn—but the butterflies leapt and fluttered with anticipation, not dread. He'd told himself and all the advice-givers he'd stay strong in the faith, but somewhere deep down, he expected to go a little wild.

His first day, he walked into the dorm room he'd be sharing with one Daren Slovak, and promptly put his foot in his mouth. "You're black."

Although Daren's eyes glinted more copper than brown, and—even wet—his hair hung around his face and shoulders in loose, auburn curls, Daren's skin shone richly dark against the pale blue towel wrapped around his waist.

"Well," Daren said quietly with a smile that looked a little sad, "kind of dark reddish brown, really, don't you think?"

*Gunner Schiller you idiot!* Gunny kept the self-scolding silent, and said out loud, "I am so sorry." Then he added, "And yes," which might have been foolish but was honest. Gunny, whose entire life had been spent around wood products, thanks to his father's business, couldn't help but compare Daren's skin to the madrone wood they occasionally used for trim on special orders.

Dark, dark red, with tight black marbling creating a misty undertone. Beautiful wood... *and beautiful skin.*

He didn't wonder where that thought had come from, because he was too busy panicking about the three twitches his dick surprised him with when he thought it. He breathed deep, wrote it off to the fact that he wasn't used to thinking about bare skin at all, his church being all about modesty and chastity. He even had sisters named for each of those virtues. He turned away as Daren dropped his towel to pull on briefs and jeans. Hoisting his backpack toward one of the beds to indicate it, Gunny said, "Is this the empty one?"

"Yes." Daren zipped, then stepped over to pick up a couple of Gunny's boxes and set them down near Gunny's closet. Then he stood up and waited for Gunny to face him. He held out his hand, looking Gunny straight in the eye with an honest, forgiving smile. "I'm Daren Slovak. To answer your curiosity about a Slovak being black, my mother is from Cameroon."

Gunny shook hands with a firm, friendly grip, and said, "Gunner Schiller, from a very white place in North Dakota. I know what I said was offensive, and I'm sorry. Honestly, I don't know why I was so surprised."

"It's okay, Gunner. I'm happy to meet you."

"Likewise, and call me Gunny."

Every day for the next month, Gunny and Daren had grown closer, sharing a couple of general-studies classes, bad jokes, movies and music, lots of pizza and ramen, and even some deeply personal conversations.

Gunny had grown used to his penis having an occasional, inexplicable but not unpleasant, burst of energy when he was enjoying Daren's company. Or when he caught sight of more than the usual amount of Daren's smooth skin. He ignored it, along with some low-key guilt over little sins like drinking and trying pot, avoiding going home for visits, and watching the occasional porn video.

Walking on the wild side, he also avoided his twin sister, Faith, who'd come to the U at the same time as Gunny, and *didn't* avoid going home. She might report to their father if she knew about Gunny's drinking, his smoker friends, his missing class due to a hangover, or his occasional commission—while in the shower—of the sin of masturbation. Admittedly, he didn't know how she'd find out about the latter, but better to just stay away from her anyway.

Being a wild man but keeping it secret was like walking a tightrope without a balance bar. The danger filled Gunny with quiet but insistent exhilaration.

By the time Halloween rolled around, conservative, respectable, reserved Gunner Schiller from North Dakota had gained a reputation as a partier. He'd even had sex with women on two occasions at parties. He didn't really remember much about that. The memory lapse might have been about booze, but truthfully he hadn't been all that drunk either time, so he thought it was mostly because the act itself hadn't been as memorable as he'd expected. The idea of sex excited him, but honestly, the women's bodies and efforts just didn't. *Oh well*, he'd thought after the second try, *you live and learn.*

Halloween night was to be one big mobile party. Gunny had bowed to popular opinion and decided he wouldn't be any more damned to hell than he already was if he dressed up, so he decided to go all out and be Satan for an evening. Tall, lithe, Daren would go as Cher, wearing a close copy of one of her signature racy outfits. Gunny was all for that idea, and he told himself that was because he'd heard music-major Daren sing Cher songs at Karaoke, and he did it beautifully—the costume just made sense.

They were joined by a pair of their more raucous acquaintances—Johnny Langdon dressed as the Lord of the Hunt, and his brother Benny, who refused to dress up at all with the exception of donning suspenders and pretending to smoke a stogie all night. Together they started the evening at a Karaoke bar within walking distance from their home base. They ordered drinks with their fake ID and maybe the costumes helped them get away with it. But it was early in the evening, and Daren's first turn at the mike came up before he or Gunny—who still tried to pace himself in an effort to reduce guilt over the sin of drunkenness—hadn't had more than a sip. Oddly, Daren seemed more self-conscious singing "Love is the Groove" than Gunny remembered him being the last time he'd done the Karaoke thing. *Looking* like Cher—and Gunny had to admit Daren, in many ways, pulled that off quite well—evidently made him self-conscious about *singing* like her.

Although, honestly, Daren didn't sing like Cher. He sang like Daren, his voice tenor but enriched with overtones from all the registers, his style strong like Cher's but, to Gunny's inexpert but attentive ear, perhaps differently nuanced.

Gunny hadn't really known a lot about Cher until he'd started rooming with Daren, who called the pop goddess his patron saint. In his new, wild-with-reservations life, Cher's music seemed to fit right in with the parties and booze and pot, all of which swirled around a central core of Daren. Gunny knew Daren was at the heart of his changes, the centrifuge that had sent everything whirling, and that was okay. He figured he'd give himself a year to spin to the outside, and then settle back down—no doubt without Daren in his life. Meanwhile he gave himself over.

That Halloween night, when Daren came off the Karaoke stage after "Love is the Groove" looking down and maybe even embarrassed, Gunny had been mystified by his own need to comfort him. He'd been schooled all his life to think a man's emotions were his own problem, and he had no reason to believe—or sense—that Daren wouldn't be just fine once he manned up. But he'd finished a hard drink by then, and that might have been why he even noticed Daren might need comfort. Not knowing the best way to go about such a not-so-macho thing, he ordered shots all around and challenged Daren to keep up with him.

Daren didn't try to do that, but he did drink, and he did loosen up, and by the time his second turn for

Karaoke came up, he was a lot more relaxed. Relaxed enough—or drunk enough—to trip on the top step of the stage. He recovered with a giggle, though and stood at the mic, gazing out at the audience with sultry eyes before launching into "Taxi Taxi." Daren's performance seemed loose and tight in all the right places and it mesmerized Gunny.

As he walked back to the table where his friends sat waiting, with applause for his performance echoing in his ears, Daren felt power coursing through his veins. He was high on it as he'd never been before, and the feeling so far surpassed the booze that Gunny had tried to get him drunk on that he didn't even want to sit back down. He needed to move.

"Let's go," he said, looking at Jimmy but oh-so-aware of Gunny's hungry look. Daren *didn't* know what that look really meant, but he liked it, and he thought he might have just made a discovery about himself that had been a long time coming.

Or maybe several discoveries, all because he liked that look. A lot. He liked knowing he'd affected Gunny by his drag Karaoke—by his look and his voice and his walk, all of which were different from, but somehow part of, everyday Daren. He liked that it made him want to get up next to Gunny and move, and he loved the feeling—the certainty—that Gunny would want that too. And that particular desire was all about sex.

*I'm gay*, he thought.

He laughed a little because how the hell had he not known that? Although... maybe he had. And then, biting his full, red-painted bottom lip and wiggling his ass a bit just for the joy of it, he thought it again. *I'm fucking gay...*

*And that's fabulous!*

The rest of the festivities that night went by in a blur. Daren sang at a couple of parties, played a racy board game, and yes, drank too much, all the while getting close to Gunny whenever he could. He never got quite so drunk that he wasn't in control, but perhaps, he admitted, he was a little past the point of good sense, because he knew Gunny was basically an innocent—or at least a naïve soul. Gunny *was* drunker than was strictly healthy, and right then Daren had some power over him. For a while, he enjoyed playing him like a fish on the line.

But when they'd left the last party, said goodbye to Ronnie and Jimmy outside their residence hall, and walked halfway back to their dorm in a steady, cool rain, Daren sobered and he didn't feel like *toying* with Gunny anymore. He wondered for a moment if Gunny really did want him, but then he realized wondering that was a little dishonest. He could see Gunny's desire, feel it. He could damn well *smell* it. But then he asked himself a more honest question. Would Gunny want him with his clothes off the same way he did when he was in drag?

Because if the answer was no, then Daren didn't want to want Gunny.

Alcohol haze had thinned to a barely distorting mist by the time Gunny followed Daren into their dorm room and closed and locked the door. He leaned back against it, staring at Daren, barely able to keep enough breath in his lungs to ask Daren for what he wanted—or *needed*.

"Hey," he panted. "Would you do it again? Sing, I mean... here, like you did at the bar... for... for me?"

Daren's red, ripe, plump lips made an O as he breathed out, and then a smile took them and lit up his eyes. "Okay.... Give me a minute." Before he shut the bathroom door behind him, he leaned out and said, "You might as well get comfortable, right?"

Gunny wasn't comfortable. He was about as uncomfortable as a North Dakota Seventh Day Adventist boy could be, with his dick more than half-hard just thinking about Daren moving that lithe brown body as he sang, imagining the way that almost female but ever-so-male, smooth yet throaty voice would wash over him as he sat watching. Because he was far more comfortable at the moment with fewer clothes, he stripped his Satan costume, though he forgot about the horns on his head. Thirsty, he twisted the top off a half-drank bottle of water on his night table, and guzzled it, then plopped down on his bed to wait.

When Daren came out of the bathroom, he'd fixed his makeup and hair, and he'd left his wrap behind. Now, he wore only black fishnet hose and the low-necked, hi-cut, one-piece leotard of his costume. The pale night-light in the room cast sliding highlights over its silver sheen fabric as Daren moved to stand front and center, not more than five feet from Gunny.

He left the music off and sang "All or Nothing" unaccompanied, low and slow at the start. Sometimes he almost spoke the words as if they were part of a conversation he was having with Gunny. Soon, though, Daren seemed swept up in the impatient need the lyrics spoke of, and his voice soared through the melody. He started to move, to sway and dance, and even without the song's usual percussive background sound, Gunny heard the beat driving hard, his pulse marking the time loud in his ears. But when he got to the last few lines, Daren lingered over them, sang them with more breath than sound, all the while holding Gunny's eyes with his own. The very last word, "Now," Daren whispered twice into the silent, dim-lit room.

Gunny felt its impact like twin stealth missiles—one to the groin, and one to the heart.

Challenge or plea, Gunny didn't know. Either way, the only possible response was "yes." He said it, and then somehow, without knowing he'd even moved, he had Daren's long hair wrapped in his fist, and he was kissing those perfect lips, holding Daren tight against his body, feeling Daren's response, and wanting skin with a passion he'd never suspected lived inside him.

**Read more of Gunny and Darren's magical holiday romance!**

# BOOKS BY LOU SYLVRE

**Suspenseful Romance by Lou Sylvre**

*VASQUEZ AND JAMES SERIES
Suspense/Romance from Changeling Press (Series 1 in the Vasquez Universe)
Volume One: *When badass meets artist, sparks and bullets fly. Blazing romance, chilling suspense, enduring love...*
Loving Luki Vasquez
Delsyn's Blues
Finding Jackie
Volume Two: *For badass Luki and artist Sonny, troubles strike, romance sizzles, love endures, a family is made.*
Saving Sonny James
Yes (a novella)
Because of Jade

*VASQUEZ INC SERIES
Suspense/Romance from Changeling Press (Series 2 in the Vasquez Universe)
*Gay American Dom with a fabulous sub juggles romance and bondage with police and security work.*
A Shot of J&B
A Shot of Fear
A Shot at Living
A Shot at Perfect

A Shot of Trust
A Shot of Courage
A Shot in Darkness, *coming January, 2021!*

**Holiday Romance by Lou Sylvre**

Falling Snow on Snow
The Holiday Home Hotel

**by Lou Sylvre and Anne Barwell**

Sunset at Pencarrow (JMS Books)—Contemporary New Zealand

The Harp and the Sea (NineStar Press)—Historical Scotland Fantasy

# ABOUT LOU SYLVRE

Lou Sylvre hails from southern California but now lives and writes on the rainy side of Washington State. When she's not writing, she's reading fiction from nearly every genre, romance in all its tints and shades, and the occasional book about history, physics, or police procedure. Her personal assistant is Boudreau, a large cat who never outgrew his kitten meow. She plays guitar (mostly where people can't hear her), and she loves to sing. She's usually smiling and laughs too much, some say. She loves her family, her friends, the felines Boudreau, Nibbles and The Lady George, a little dog named Joe, and (in random order) coffee, chocolate, sunshine, and wild roses, among other things.

Hearing from a reader invariably brightens her day. Drop her a line at louwrites@gmail.com.

Sign up for Lou Sylvre's newsletter.
https://www.subscribepage.com/l6z9j1_sylvre_2

Find Lou Sylvre on the Web
https://www.facebook.com/AuthorLouSylvre/
https://twitter.com/Sylvre
http://www.sylvre.rainbow-gate.com

CPSIA information can be obtained
at www.ICGtesting.com
Printed in the USA
BVHW031733210921
617208BV00001B/9